BULBUL SHARMA,  woodcuts, is the author c the enormously popular *Now That I'm Fifty* and *The Anger of Aubergines*. She has also written books on birds and trees for children. She teaches art to children with special needs.

Travels With My Aunts

BULBUL SHARMA

women
UNLIMITED
an associate of
kali for women

Travels With My Aunts
was first published in India in 2015
by
Women Unlimited
(an associate of Kali for Women)
7/10, First Floor, Sarvapriya Vihar
New Delhi 110016
www.womenunlimited.net

ISBN: 978-81-88965-99-1

Cover design: Neelima Rao

Typeset by Eleven Arts, Delhi–110035

To
my mother, Meera Mukherjee
—a great storyteller

Contents

Mayadevi's London Yatra

THE DAY MAYADEVI TURNED SIXTY-EIGHT, SEVENTY OR SEVENTY-five (her date of birth was an ever-changing fact linked to her moods), she decided to go to London. Everyone in the family was stunned when she announced this, but no one dared to speak out because the old lady ruled over the entire three-storied house with a quiet reign of terror. Whenever she decided to do something, her three sons and their wives quickly agreed, since they had learnt slowly and bitterly, over the years, that no one questioned the old lady's whims.

Though there was no need for Mayadevi to give an explanation to her submissive and docile family, she still called her sons and gave her reasons for undertaking such an unusual journey at her age. 'I want to see Amit before I die.' This eldest son of hers had gone to England to study when he was eighteen years old and had never returned to India since then. He wrote to his mother on the fifteenth of every month and sent her money regularly, along with many expensive but useless presents, but did not come home to see her because he had an acute phobia of flying. He had travelled to England by ship in 1948, and once he had landed there after a traumatic and unpleasant journey, he never stepped out of the safety of the island for the next forty years. There had been a few short, tension-filled holiday trips to France and to Italy, but these were either by train or by boat. Around every October, as the Puja season approached, he promised his mother that this year he would take the plunge and get into an aircraft and come to Calcutta, but his nerve failed him with reassuring regularity each time.

'The wretched boy was always a sissy. He could never cross the road if a cow was standing in the middle. Lizards frightened him and rats made him scream even when he was fifteen years old. I will shame him by going to London—to his very doorstep, even if I have to bathe in the Ganga a hundred times after I return,' the old lady declared, and the sons, who thought it a very foolish idea, nodded their agreement as they had done all their lives.

Once the momentous decision had been taken, Mayadevi began planning for her journey on a warlike footing. She first applied for a passport and visa, but filled in the forms with a lot of arguments and protests because she did not like the impertinent questions the government dared ask her. Once that was over, she bought a big register and wrote down her plan of action step by step.

Then she decided to attack the English language. Though Mayadevi had never been to school, she could read and write Bengali fluently and was far better read than her graduate, accountant sons. She could understand simple sentences in English but had never spoken the language to anyone in her entire life since the occasion had never risen. Now she hunted out a tattered old English primer which belonged to one of her grandchildren, and every morning, after she had finished her puja, folded her Gita away safely and distributed the sanctified sweets, she sat down to study this jam-stained old book. The household, usually peaceful and quiet in the mornings, was now filled with Mayadevi's strange rendering of the English primer. Sitting cross-legged on the floor and rocking herself backwards and forward, she read each line over and over again in a musical singsong as if she were chanting a sacred verse. Then she would suddenly stop and ask herself questions. 'Did Jack fetch the bucket?' she would ask in an accusing tone, and then reply, 'No, Jane fetched the bucket.' She would get up once in a while, adjust her spectacles and take a short walk around the room, holding the closed book near her chest as she had seen her grandson do when he was memorizing a text.

The servants did not dare come near the study area but watched her nervously from the kitchen doorway. They were sure she was learning English only to terrorize them more effectively. 'At her age she should be only reading the Gita, not repeating jack-jack-jack like a parrot,' they said, but only when within the safety of the servants quarters. The lesson unnerved the cook so much that he stopped fiddling with the marketing accounts and turned honest, in case the old lady, armed with the English language, caught him out. The daughters-in-law too found the lessons very odd and giggled quietly in their bedrooms, but they were careful to put on a serious face when they came anywhere near the vicinity of the English lessons. The sons also kept their distance from their mother after their eager efforts to help her with her English pronunciation had met with a cold rebuff. 'For sixty years I have managed this house and my life without any help from you or your late father. I do not have any wish to start now,' she said, dismissing them with a regal wave of the tattered book.

So she carried on learning the primer and the household not only got used to the strange sounds, but caught the infectious tone too and the servants began humming 'Jack and Jill' as they went about their chores. Within a few weeks, Mayadevi had finished the primer and graduated to more difficult books. She now carried on long conversations with herself to air her newly acquired knowledge of English, and as the days went by, the characters from the primer, the *Teach Yourself English in 21 Days* and other books got mixed up with each other in the most unfortunate, tangled relationships. 'Did Jane go to the grocer's shop alone? No, Mr Smith went too.' 'Mrs Smith is sitting on the bench in the garden with Jack. She is smoking a pipe. How are you, Jack? Quite well, thank you. Where is the tramway?' her voice would drone endlessly till she had learnt all the words in each and every book by heart and so had the rest of the household.

Now there were only three months left for the date of departure and Mayadevi went into the next stage of her travel preparations for the great journey which had been named London Yatra by her family, though, of course, behind her back. 'Now I am going to wear shoes,' she announced and ordered one of her sons to get her a pair of black canvas shoes and six pairs of white cotton socks. Mayadevi had always walked barefoot in the house and worn slippers on the rare occasions she went out to visit. The no. 3 blue rubber slippers lasted her for five years at least, and though they hardly ever stepped on the road, they were washed every day with soap. But in England, these faithful slippers would not do, and so Mayadevi reluctantly and with a martyred air, forced her thin, arthritic feet into her first pair of shoes. For one hour in the morning, after the English lessons, and then another hour after her evening tea, the old lady practised walking in her new shoes. Like an egret stepping out on clumsy, mud-covered feet, the white-clad figure paced up and down the house, accompanied by a rhythmic squeaking of rubber. Soon there were large blisters on her feet, but Mayadevi carried on the struggle like a seasoned warrior and no one heard her expel a single sigh ever. Her sons admired her from a distance, but did not dare to praise her, since they knew she distrusted flattery of any kind and always said, 'Say what you want from me and leave out the butter.' So no one ever praised her, and came straight to the point when asking for favours.

When there was only one month left for the departure, Mayadevi wrote to her son in England and informed him of her plans. He instantly went into a severe panic and telephoned her, which he had rarely done in the last forty years. 'Ma, please do not undertake such a dangerous journey. Planes are crashing all the time. You can be hijacked to Libya. Air travel is really unsafe now. You wait, I will definitely come home by ship next Puja,' he screamed hysterically over the bad line.

Mayadevi listened to him patiently and then replied, 'I may be dead by next Puja. My ticket has been bought. You will come and receive me at the airport and make sure you come alone and not with that giant wife of yours,' she said and put the phone down firmly though she could hear her son's voice still cackling on the line. From then on, there was total silence from across the ocean, but that did not bother the old lady and she now moved into the final preparations for the London Yatra. She started visiting her relatives one by one and each one was informed of the travel plans personally by her, just as if she was following the norm for issuing wedding invitations. She did not sit for long in any house but just gave a brief outline of why she was going to England and then left without accepting any tea or even a glass of water. The relatives were surprised not only by this flying visit, like royalty, but also by the fact that she chose to tell them why she was going. 'The old battleaxe is losing her strength. Getting soft in the head now,' they said, but were secretly pleased that she had condescended to visit them.

After this came the most important stage. One morning, the old lady called her sons and the family priest for a meeting. The daughters-in-law and the servants, not invited, took turns to listen at the door. 'In case I die in that land, though god will never do such a thing to me, bring my body back immediately, before they contaminate it. Then see that all the rituals of purification are done properly,' she said, fixing the priest with such an unblinking, cold look that he began to tremble with fear and could not help thinking that the old lady had died already and was watching him from heaven. Once the plans of how to deal with her dead person had been discussed to her satisfaction, Mayadevi gave them detailed instructions for the purification rites she, if returned alive, would go through on the very day she came back.

'There is a week-long penance to be done, brahmins are to be fed and the entire house is to be washed with water from the Ganga. So see that you take leave from office, all of you,' she said to the sons, who understood the importance of the occasion and readily nodded their heads, hoping the meeting had finally ended.

Now only one week was left for the date of departure. A large, battered suitcase, which had been a part of Mayadevi's impressive dowry when she came to this house as a fifteen-year-old bride, was brought out from the dark corners of the storeroom and Mayadevi began packing. Six white cotton saris, six petticoats and an equal number of blouses, one white sweater and a grey shawl, along with a small, red cloth bag for her Gita and her prayer beads, and a plastic box for her false teeth were the only items she packed. 'Everything, except the Gita and my teeth, will be thrown away when I return, so why waste money?' she said. The suitcase was packed and ready five days in advance and left on top of the stairs like a coveted trophy. Everyone who came or left the house would trip over it but not a murmur of protest was heard. In fact, the servants proudly dusted it every day and the children approached it with awe.

Then finally the day of departure arrived. Mayadevi got up before dawn, bathed and went into her prayer room. She knelt before the gods and whispered, 'Give me strength to endure this ordeal and let me not die in that land. I promise to make you new ornaments of gold when I return. Please bring me back safely to you.' She sat for a long time in that small, incense-filled room and only when the light began to stream in through the windows did she get up and go out to wake up her sons. Soon the entire household was rushing around, though there was nothing very much to do. The suitcase was dusted a few times and the children made to touch their grandmother's feet every time they passed her way. The sons kept clearing their throats and looking at their watches. 'Has she got everything?' they muttered, but not too loudly, since none of them wanted to go and check. Mayadevi packed five large packets of puffed rice in a cloth bundle and filled up her grandson's plastic water bottle. This was all that Mayadevi was going to eat for the next twelve hours, because she was not going to touch any food 'that god knows who had touched'. The day passed quickly as visitors came to say goodbye. Each one admired the suitcase and, after bumping into it, remarked how light it was. The plane left at twelve o'clock at night, but Mayadevi and her sons were already at the airport four hours before that. They sat solemnly in a row and watched the clock now, instead of their wristwatches. They had never before spent such a concentrated and confined time with their mother and were finding it very difficult to sit so close to her on the plastic chairs. They took care to change places so that no one had to sit for too long near her and each brother could get some respite. Once in a while, Mayadevi spoke to give some last-minute instructions. Her sons only nodded and cleared their throats once again. At last the flight was announced. The old lady lifted her head and listened carefully. Suddenly one of her sons got carried away by emotion and tried to give his mother a few travel tips, but she got up quietly and joined the long queue of passengers weaving their way to check in. One by one, the sons, bending with difficulty under their middle-age spreads, touched their mother's feet. She blessed them with a rarely seen gentle smile, and as they stood like orphans, she sailed out of their vision and into the gaping door of the security area. The sons were not worried about their aged mother. They only wondered how England would cope.

It was raining when the plane landed in London. A flicker of worry crossed Mayadevi's mind as she wondered whether her still uncertain shoe-walking ability would be able to manage the wet ground. 'It will have to be done,' she said to herself, looking down sternly at the shiny black shoes, as if ordering them to obey her. She adjusted her sari, still crisp and starched after twelve hours, and got ready to leave the plane. Throughout the flight she had sat ramrod straight and when the air hostess had offered to adjust her seat to a more comfortable, reclining position, she had said, 'Why I sit like that? I am not sick,' in a sharp voice, freezing the pretty young hostess's smile before it could even begin. She ignored the old lady after that but could not help glancing at the odd white-covered head each time she passed her seat.

Mayadevi's neighbour too had stopped talking to her before they had even crossed the Hindukush mountains and now pointedly looked the other way. She had tried to be friendly and helpful and had showed the old lady how to fasten her seatbelt. Mayadevi at first did not say a word and the younger girl thought she was just shy about not being able to speak English and became even more friendly. 'Everyone was so kind to me in India. Even though the people are so poor, they have such large hearts,' she said, warming up to the subject, happily rehearsing what she was going to say many times over when she reached home, when suddenly Mayadevi opened her mouth for the first time and said, 'Why they not be kind? They lick white people's shoes two hundred years and now it become bad habit like drinking and smoking.' The girl was shocked. Never in her six months' stay in India, during which she had travelled the length and breadth of the country, staying only with families, since one could get to know 'real India' that way, and also hotels were so expensive, but she had never ever been met with such rudeness. She was gathering her wits to say something sharp in reply, when Mayadevi told her to take her elbow off the armrest. 'I do not want you to touch my sari,' she said. After that they sat silently, a cold wall between them, for the next twelve hours.

When the air hostess came with the meals, Mayadevi shook her head firmly and also crossed her hands over her lap, in the traditional manner of refusing food at Bengali feasts, to doubly confirm her refusal. She then watched the young girl eat her meal and stared at her with an expression of such distaste that the poor girl left her food half-eaten, though she was enjoying the European meal, even a plastic-covered, airline one, after six months of endless dal and chappatis. Once in a while, Mayadevi would eat a handful of puffed rice and take a few sips of water from her plastic bottle. The bundle containing the rice and the water bottle had been carried close to her body throughout the journey, and when the security men at the airport had asked her to send it through the X-ray machine, she had clung to the bundle like a lioness to her cubs and said, 'Touch it and I will throw it in your face. I will starve for the next twelve hours, and if I die, you and your next fourteen generations will have the sin of an old woman's death on your heads.' The security men, trained only to deal with terrorists, did not know how to handle this woman and allowed the old lady and her clumsy bundle to pass without any checking. Actually Mayadevi did not really need the rice and could easily have stayed without food for many hours at a stretch, since she had been fasting for some auspicious day or the other from the time she was a young girl and her stomach was quite used to stern starvation regimes. But now that the plane was about to land, it suddenly gave a loud rumble of protest, startling Mayadevi by this uncharacteristic rebellion. The young girl heard the grumblings too and allowed herself a small, mean smile. 'Old cow, hope she has a bad time here,' she thought, but then immediately felt guilty and filled up Mayadevi's landing form for her. Mayadevi never said a 'thank you', and as soon as the plane came to a halt, she shot up from her seat. She marched down the aisle, clutching her food bundle close to her body so that no one could contaminate it by touching it and was the first passenger to get out of the aircraft. She then slowed down and attached herself to a group of Indian passengers who had also just come off the plane. She followed them closely, but when they reached the immigration area and began queuing up, she walked past them and planted herself firmly at the head of the line. No one could ask an old lady to move back, and even if someone had, Mayadevi had her steely look ready. The young blonde man at the immigration smiled at her kindly, even though it was against his principles to smile at immigrants or visitors of any hue. In return for the rare grin, he received the famous dead-fish stare, under which innumerable men and women of Calcutta, young and old, had quelled. The young official felt sheepish for no reason at all and quickly called for an interpreter, an almost SOS urgency creeping into his voice.

'I speak English. You speak English with me,' Mayadevi said clearly.

The immigration official cleared his throat and said, 'How long do you plan to stay in UK?', and when Mayadevi said nothing, he repeated the question, adding a 'Madam' this time.

'No need to say again, again. I answer you. I stay in this land one week only. Not a day longer. You can tell your Queen Victoria,' said Mayadevi.

The stunned official stamped her passport with a resounding thump and waved her on as fast as he could. 'This is one old bird who is not lying to me. Won't ever catch her working in Selfridges, for sure,' he said and laughed nervously as if some ordeal had been passed.

Mayadevi again followed the passengers she had marked out and made sure they collected her suitcase and carried it for her in their trolley. Her son was waiting for her outside when she finally emerged, but even though she saw him at once, she gave no sign that she recognized him.

The sixty-year-old, extremely successful dentist, member of the Royal College of Dentists and a very old London club, did not dare raise his arm and wave to his mother. She walked towards him slowly, and after she reached him, stood staring at him as if he were a total stranger. The son lurched forward and made an awkward, half-bending movement to touch his mother's feet but at the same time surreptitiously tried to look as if he was tying his shoelaces. Mayadevi, who was on full alert, her eyes carefully scrutinizing her son for faults, pounced like an eagle on the first wrong move. 'Ashamed to touch your mother's feet now, are you? A mother who has not long to live but even then has travelled such a great distance, fasting for twelve hours, sitting with all kinds of half-castes so that she can see her son,' she hissed. Amit, who was well known in the dentists' circles for his dry, sharp wit, was about to defend himself with a few crisp, well-chosen words, but before he could speak, something clicked inside him. As he looked into that old lined face, an irrational fear jolted his memory and he said in a whining, childish voice, 'No, Ma ... I ... so many people here,' he stammered helplessly. Now that she had established the old family hierarchy in the correct order, Mayadevi told her son to pick up her suitcase and take her to his home. Though the mother and son had not seen each other for forty years, they drove to the semi-detached house in the beautiful, green, tree-lined suburbs in unbroken, stony silence. The mother asked no questions and the son offered no explanations, because he somehow felt that she knew everything about him already and disapproved strongly. When they reached home, Mayadevi got out of the car in a suspicious, stealthy manner as if she was expecting hidden traps in the neatly laid out garden. Mother and son entered the house like two mourners, and when his wife came out of the kitchen to greet them, Amit almost burst into tears with relief.

'Welcome to England, Mrs Banerjee. Hope you had a nice flight,' Martha, Amit's wife, said cheerfully. Mayadevi looked up at her tall, large-boned daughter-in-law through the top of her spectacles for a few long, uncomfortable seconds and then said, 'I want to wash hands. Everything so dirty.' Martha's plain, good-natured face showed a brief flicker of surprise but she beamed at her mother-in-law and said, 'Come and see your room and then we will have a nice cup of tea. Hope you like the new curtains we put up for you. Amit did not know what your favourite colour was, so I chose blue,' she prattled on, her voice full of genuine affection for the old lady she had never met before. Amit crept up to shelter behind his wife's ample frame as his mother examined the room, and cringed each time Martha went too close to her. He knew what would happen if Martha touched her by mistake. 'Are you feeling cold? Shall I turn up the central heating?' asked Martha, suddenly feeling the cold herself. Though Mayadevi was shivering in her thin cotton sari, she said, 'Not cold, only wash hands, so much dirty.' Martha quickly led her to the bathroom, gaily decorated with trailing plants and fluffy rugs. Mayadevi slammed the door shut on Martha's smiling face and began to wash her hands. First she washed the taps thoroughly and then she began rinsing the soap, though it was a brand new one. Then she finally washed her hands meticulously four times in a row. When she had finished, she turned the tap off with her elbow, so as not to touch the tap again. She dried her hands by shaking them about in the air, looking scornfully, as she did so, at the pretty, flowered hand towels Martha had put out for her. Then she went out to search for her son. 'How will I bathe in that jungle you call bathroom? Why has she put carpets in the bathroom? To hide the dirty floor?' she charged with full force, happy to have found something to complain about so quickly.

'Ma, she will hear you,' said Amit, glancing nervously at the kitchen door, even though they were speaking in Bengali. 'You must be tired. Why don't you eat the rice I have made for you and go to sleep now?' he said, desperately hoping she would agree. Surprisingly she did. 'If you are telling the truth that she did not make it,' was the only half-hearted resistance she put up and followed him to the kitchen. 'I cooked it, Ma. She did not even touch it. I am not lying to you,' he said and flushed when he saw Martha watching him, even though he knew she could not understand what he had said. But Mayadevi made sure that the message had got through by giving her a triumphant look. She took out her false teeth with a sharp, satisfied click and sat down to eat. The meal, a bowl of overcooked rice and a muddy brown dal, was consumed quickly and noisily as Mayadevi chewed with her gums, and when she had finished, she took her plate to the sink and washed it carefully twice. She shook it dry by waving it in the air and then kept it as far away as possible from the other plates and dishes. Martha's friendly smile had by now faded to a bewildered, confused look and she stood silently, watching the water from the plate drip all over her hospital-like, sparkling-clean kitchen floor. But she did not know what to do or say. Amit stood next to her, wearing the expression of a sad, unhappy man, expecting even worse times ahead.

Mayadevi, quite content now with the way things had gone so far, left them both and went to her room. She dragged the bedcover off the bed, spread it on the floor, and then, after saying her prayers, fell fast asleep at once. She woke up in the middle of the night and sat bolt upright. The greyish-yellow streetlight streamed in through the window and the sky outside was a lighter shade than she had ever seen. Calcutta seemed very far away. 'God forgive me, I will return soon,' said Mayadevi, feeling lonely for the first time in her long, solitary life.

The next day passed very much like the first one, only Mayadevi cooked the food for herself and Amit. He felt guilty about not eating with Martha but his mother's contemptuous, 'Ha! A slave to his wife,' plus the delicious fragrance of long-forgotten, favourite dishes, compelled him to sit down and eat with his mother every evening as he came back from work. Martha never complained and he did not dare to ask her what they both did during the day, but he got the answer anyway, judging by the new, unhappy lines on his wife's forever-cheerful face. Like two boxing champions trapped in a ring, Martha and Mayadevi circled around the house, avoiding each other but at the same time keeping a wary eye on what the other person was doing. The old lady would listen as her daughter-in-law went about doing her housework and then she would tiptoe out, her eyes gleaming like a fault-finding laser beam, to check out her work. She opened drawers, peered under the beds and ran her fingers over the windowpanes. But she could not find any dust or cobwebs, as she did on her weekly checking rounds in her house in Calcutta. Angry and bored, Mayadevi took to sitting in her bedroom in sullen silence for the entire day. Martha did try from time to time to make friendly overtures but each time she met a solid wall of silent rebuff. Mayadevi would shut her eyes tightly and pretend to chant her prayers every time her daughter-in-law looked into her room. She never wanted to go out to look at the shops, watch television or drink tea, and Martha could not think of anything else to cajole the old lady out of the room.

Slowly the six days of unspoken tension passed, and Mayadevi happily began packing her bag once more. 'Thank god, it is over, the wretched trip,' she muttered. The last day of the visit was a Saturday, and Amit had taken the day off from his clinic. He had been hoping that some emergency would crop up and he would have to rush to the clinic, but he knew very well that it was a foolish thought and a dentist had no crisis of broken molars or sudden cavities in his career. He decided bravely to face the situation and take his mother out shopping. Martha, her good-natured spirit still alive, offered to come along too but Amit said in a courageous voice, 'No, you rest, dear. I will take her alone,' as if he was going off to slay some dreaded dragon. But Martha insisted on coming along to give him unspoken support. They drove to the large shopping centre nearby, Mayadevi sitting at the back, spurning all friendly remarks and efforts at showing her the sights of London. When they reached the huge, glittering building, there was an embarrassing tussle in the car park. Mayadevi did not want to get out from the car.

'Why should I go to this big shop? What do I want to buy from here?' she asked her son, facing him squarely. Amit stared helplessly at the giant shopping complex with ten floors of the world's best merchandise, but he could not think of a single thing his mother could buy there. 'Well, now that we are here, let us go in. You can tell everyone at home what you saw, can't you?' he said with a wide, foolish grin, as if he was talking to a child. Mayadevi snorted in the haughty, dignified way only she could. But now that she had made her protest, she stepped briskly out of the car. They went into the building, and after a slight pause to fight the escalator, where Mayadevi's sari got stuck in the gap between the steps and she, thinking Amit had stepped on it, kept scolding loudly. They disentangled her and then walked straight into the fairyland of gifts, cosmetics, perfume and lingerie department.

Mayadevi suddenly stood still. She felt as if she had been struck by lightning. In her entire seventy-five-odd years, she had never seen a world like this. Hundreds of bright lights gleamed everywhere she looked. Dazzling, blinding mirrors as tall as trees, and walls that had solid gold lamps on them. There were countless mysterious, colourful objects she could not recognize, on every glossy surface. Silken bits of lace were draped all over glass shelves and though they had an odd shape like two cups, Mayadevi, who had never worn any undergarments like most other women of her age, thought they were the most beautiful lace decorations. She could smell the fragrance drifting up from the glittering glass bottles filled with magical potions. It was the most powerful and sweet incense she had ever smelt. There were jewels as big as eggs in boxes that shone with silver and gold threads. Mayadevi felt that she had died and come to heaven, only the people were wrong. 'There should have been our gods and goddesses in this paradise, not these pale humans,' she said softly to herself, not moving in case it was a dream. Her daughter-in-law suddenly understood what had happened to the old lady. She took her arm and gently guided her through the maze-like, narrow lanes of the department store, overflowing with gleaming merchandise. For once Mayadevi did not flinch at her touch and followed Martha meekly as if she was a celestial maiden guiding her in paradise.

'I think we should get her a nice warm jumper, Amit,' Martha said to her husband, who had not yet noticed the sudden change in his mother. They went to the women's department and Martha picked up a pale-blue cardigan. 'No, no, only white,' whispered Mayadevi still in a trance. Martha found a fluffy white one quickly and also a lacy white shawl to go with it. She presented them both to the old lady with a friendly smile. But this gift was a greater shock for Mayadevi than seeing the big department store, in all its glory, for the first time. Her late husband, her many children and countless relatives had always given her what she had asked for, but no one had ever given her a present. Her steely eyes, unused to crying, became almost blind with tears, and through the blur she took Martha's hand and shook it as she had seen people in her phrase book do. 'Good girl, very well, thank you,' she said to her daughter-in-law, showering her with the polite words she knew in English.

By the time they reached home, Mayadevi's brief moment of weakness passed and the vision had cleared. She was her old self again, but there was a certain change in her demeanour. She did not actually smile, but her eyes lost that old freezing glance and she called Martha by name. The next day, before she left for the airport, she let Martha make her tea, and though she did not thank her when she placed the cup in front of her, Martha little knew how much sacrifice and giving it meant for the old lady. The journey to the airport was silent this time too, but not an unhappy, uncomfortable one. When the time came for Mayadevi to leave, she patted Martha's hand and said, 'When I die, you come to Calcutta for funeral. Let my fool of a son be. You come.' Then, after making sure that her son had touched her feet properly, she walked into the 'passengers only' area. She did not turn around to wave at them, though she knew she would probably never see her son again. She was content that she had done her duty and now she looked forward to the year-long penance, purifications and sacrificial rituals she would have to do to wash away the sins of the London Yatra.

Bishtupur Landing

TO FIND OUT THE REASON THAT LED TO THE SHOCKING INCIDENT when Neelima crash-landed in her husband's village in Bishtupur one morning in 1939, we have to go back ten years, when Neelima was seven years old. She was not a bright child and struggled through school, complaining bitterly against being educated. Her father, a very learned man who prided himself for his modern views on emancipation of women, was aghast at having a daughter who so vehemently wanted to remain in the dark ages. 'Mother never went to school and neither did my aunts or my cousins, and they are all very happy, so why should *I* be the only one to suffer and learn by heart hundreds of English verbs and multiplication tables?' Neelima would lament each morning to her father before she was reluctantly sent off to school. It needed a trio of servants to force her out of the house and get her into her school every day. The maid would drag her by the hand, the young servant boy would carry her bag as well as help the maid along by pushing Neelima each time she stalled. As they moved one step forward and two steps backwards like a six-legged monster, the driver would coax and cajole Neelima with bribes of sweets and promises of wonderful sights he would show her on the way.

When she reached the school gates, Neelima would dig in her heels again and stall like an obstinate, unbroken colt, and her maid would have to catch hold of both her hands and pull her all the way to her class. Her chubby legs dragging in the dust and her plaits flying like two thick streamers behind her, the seven-year-old girl would enter the prestigious girls' school in an undignified procession each morning. The teachers tried to help, but since Neelima behaved quite well after this initial protest, they let her make her daily dramatic entrance to school.

Neelima was a poor student, barely managing to pass the annual exams, but she won a prize every year for being the healthiest girl in school. There were other equally, if not more, plump, pink-cheeked girls in the school, but since Neelima's father gave the largest donation each year, the prize automatically went to his daughter. This award, instead of encouraging the girl to like her school better, made her even more unhappy, and as the time for the annual ceremony approached, her arrival at the school gates took on an almost fierce battle-like appearance. Now the maid, the driver and the young boy had to be helped by the school gatekeeper and the four of them, puffing and panting, dragged the plump girl out of the car and pushed her into the class.

On the day of the ceremony, the teachers made sure Neelima arrived an hour early, so that the unseemly struggle would be over by the time the guests arrived. The prizes were given away by the local collector's wife and this lady struck a special terror in Neelima's already overdistraught heart. For weeks before and after the ceremony, the girl would wake up screaming at night as the collector's large and ferocious-looking wife appeared regularly in her dreams, smiling toothily like a she-wolf and continuously nodding her head. The English lady, despite her formidable looks, was a mild-mannered soul and took a keen interest in the school. She always said a few kind words to each girl 'to put them at their ease and also to encourage them'. But when Neelima's turn came, the girl would tremble so much and stare at her with such large dark-shadowed eyes that the lady quickly gave her the prize and moved on to the next girl, always wondering why the school chose such a pale, nervous child as the healthiest one. 'You never know what the natives think, can you?' she said to her friends privately. Which was just as well, because she would have been very surprised to know what stormy, black thoughts went on in Neelima's mind during that brief prize-giving period. The annual event frightened her so much that it scared her for life and even now, when Neelima is an old lady, she begins to tremble when she thinks of those terrible prize-giving ceremony days, though many greater events of horror, like the Bishtupur landing, took place after that as she stumbled through life. But let's get back to earlier events. Neelima went on fighting against being schooled, and gradually, bit by bit, wore her father down. The last straw was when the maid, now quite old and frail, rebelled. She refused point blank to drag and carry the plump, sixteen-year-old Neelima, who was still winning the prize for being the healthiest girl, to school any longer.

'Get another stronger woman. I have served you well but now my arms are no longer the same. Khukumoni, god preserve her, is as strong as a young bull now and I do not have the strength to fight her any more.'

The women of the house too were on Neelima's side, since they saw no value in educating women. 'What has she learnt in all these years? She can neither embroider handkerchiefs, sing a proper tune, dress fish, nor can she pour boiling milk without spilling half of it. All she knows is how to read and write a little bit of English. Let her stay at home so that we can all have some peace in the mornings.' Her father finally allowed her to stay at home. A triumphant Neelima left school just before finishing her matric. 'Now you can get me married,' she declared, satisfied at having got her way at last, but worried, in case her father suddenly changed his mind. The father, who was now well known in his community for his forward, new thinking, was acutely embarrassed by his daughter's persistent demand to be wed. 'Wait for a while. What will people say? Just the other day I published an article on the evils of child marriage. How will I face my readers?' he cried. But Neelima, suspicious that her father might trap her into being educated at home by tutors, kept up her demand to be married off. Since, once again, she was supported by all the women of the family and most eagerly by her old maid, who was even more tired of Neelima's education than Neelima herself, the father had no choice but to give in yet again.

A disappointed man, he began, discreetly but painstakingly, searching for a husband for his daughter. Neelima, besides being an heiress, was a very pretty girl and, moreover, everyone knew about the famous prizes for health and soon a line of mothers with marriageable sons began to visit the house. While Neelima's mother entertained the mothers lavishly with homemade sweets and snacks, her father, an extremely fastidious man, dismissed the sons one by one as they failed to come up to his requirements. 'The boy should be tall, because my daughter is only 4'10" and I do not want a line of dwarfs as grandchildren. He should not be too fair; those types always have a weak stomach and keep getting boils. He should not be very rich because then he will always be going to court to settle some family dispute or the other. Most important of all, he should be at least a B.A. and be able to educate my daughter who is more or less an illiterate,' said the father to each prospective suitor or his mother. The women of the house mocked him and said, 'Why not add that he should come flying down from heaven in a golden chariot? Where on this earth will you find such a boy?' But, surprisingly, he did exist and was tracked down by Neelima's father after just one year and six months of diligent searching. Debashish was 6' tall; he had a healthy, golden-brown skin, of the colour of ripe wheat; his late father had been the headmaster of a village school; and the boy was so bright that he had studied throughout on scholarships and become a lecturer in a prestigious college. Not only that, he was a champion of women's education and had published several articles on the subject. Neelima's father could not believe he was true and wrote twice to check out the facts. Once everything was verified to his satisfaction, he relaxed and began to boast how difficult it had been to find such a boy. The women of the family, now humble and silent, listened in wonder as the wonder boy's qualifications were read out repeatedly by his self-satisfied, future father-in-law.

A date was fixed for the boy to come and see Neelima, though he had not expressed any wish to do so. Neelima's father insisted, once again trying to prove his modern views, which were constantly being thwarted by his difficult daughter. The household now began to prepare for the visit in a grand way and Neelima, till now happy about the arrangements, suddenly got cold feet and the collector's wife began appearing in her dreams once more. She took to walking about the house dusting the countless bric-a-brac in an agitated manner, followed by an even more nervous band of servants, in case she broke some precious ornament. The meeting or the viewing was to take place in a large, gloomy hall called the baithak ghar—the formal sitting-room in which no one from the family was ever allowed to sit. As a result, the room had a strong odour of moth balls, which, mingled with a faint but unmistakable smell of dead mice, produced a heady, musty aroma. The servants had tried to disguise the smell by lighting incense sticks behind all the heavy picture frames and sofas. When the boy and his uncles came into the room in a neat, orderly line, each one of them was assailed by this strange smell, but Debashish was struck so badly that he broke into a fit of sneezing. The parties waited at each end of the large room and watched him with bated breath. They could not make their formal greetings to each other till the boy had finished. But there seemed to be no end to Debashish's sneezes and the more he inhaled the musty air of the room the more powerful his sneezes became. Neelima's father, despite all his modern thinking, now began to get worried that the evil eye had fallen on the perfect, tall, dark, poor and highly educated boy he had found after such a long and tedious search. He quickly began the ceremonies and welcomed the boy's family with a flowery speech he had memorized for the occasion. The other party, relieved that the silence had at last been broken by something else besides the boy's sneezes, lobbed back their replies with equal grace and flourish, as Debashish continued in the background with his gunshot sneezes. They smiled at each other and gushed on, ignoring the boy totally.

Bit by bit, Neelima's various cousins tripped into the room to examine the boy, and despite the red, watery eyes, a sniffling and twitching nose, they liked him immediately and carried good reports back to Neelima. But Debashish's heart sank when he saw these diminutive girls standing half-hidden behind the sofa. 'Was he marrying into a family of dwarfs? Maybe his future bride would be wheeled into the room in a pram,' he thought panic-stricken. But when Neelima walked into the dark, gloomy room at last, like a ray of sunshine after a cloudy day, Debashish heaved a sigh of relief and his sneezing stopped miraculously. Neelima too, when she strained her neck, looked up high and gazed into the kind, red-rimmed eyes, now no longer felt as if she was at the prize-giving ceremony. Her knees stopped trembling and her hands did not twitch nervously to dust everything within reach.

They were married after a month with quiet pomp and everyone remarked on what a good pair the tall, dark boy and the short, fair girl made. Neelima was happy at last. She had escaped school and the collector's wife for ever. She settled down in their new home happily. She tried to learn cooking but gave it up after one week, much to Debashish's relief. Then she tried to practise her singing for a few days but the neighbours collected at her doorstep as soon as she had finished the first composition, demanding to know if her husband was beating her and if she needed their help. She had just begun to try out the new sewing machine when Debashish's uncle came and announced that Neelima would have to go to their village to meet the rest of the relatives. She immediately began to feel apprehensive. 'What if they keep me there and send me to the village school?' After all, his father had been the headmaster there. But Debashish assured her that would never happen. 'No woman in my family has ever been to school and they will certainly not send a new bride there. I tried so hard but they never even learnt to write their names. They just want to see you. Ever since my parents died, the elders of the village have been like a family to me and I must show them my wife.'

The journey to the village, which was situated somewhere beyond Khulna, was going to take at least two days, and Neelima, who had never travelled on her own anywhere, threw herself energetically into preparing for her maiden trip. She got the largest trunk out and decided to pack all her new clothes, of which there were hundreds, boxes of heavy jewellery and also all the expensive gifts she had received. She stuffed her clothes untidily into the trunk and above that threw a pile of velvet quilts, the brand new sewing machine she was so eager to tryout, a large wall clock, two lampshades and a stuffed cockatoo. She also gathered all her old dolls, which she had brought along with her impressive dowry to her husband's house, and laid them out like corpses on top of the bulging trunk. Debashish was stunned when his young bride proudly displayed the packed trunk to him. 'How did you manage to get that stuffed bird in?' was all that he could think of saying.

For the next few days, he gradually unpacked the trunk, wiping his wife's tears and soothing her as each unnecessary item was taken out. One by one they went, till only a few clothes and old toys were left at the bottom of the trunk, and then Neelima suddenly showed her old mulish spirit and turned obstinate. She insisted on taking with her three old dolls that danced and sang when you wound them up. These expensive English dolls were her favourites out of the many bribes she had received from her father to go to school, and Neelima was not going to leave them behind. Her husband did not want to argue with his eighteen-year-old wife and let her repack the dolls.

They left the next evening by train, along with the uncle and two widowed aunts, who suddenly turned up from nowhere. Neelima's father had wanted to send a few servants with them, but Debashish said their village hut was too small for so many people and added firmly that Neelima must learn to manage on her own now, and live how people of the villages lived. The learned gentleman was very impressed and quickly repeated what his son-in-law had said to all his friends. He did not dare come to the station either, but told the stationmaster to help them. Unaware of the hidden helping hand, Debashish was surprised how easily they managed to get into an empty compartment. The aunts quickly spread their bedding out on the seats. Neelima was made to take off all her gold jewellery and the two aunts wrapped it up in a dirty cloth bundle. There was a minor tussle as to which aunt would keep this bundle under her head and sleep, and finally the younger of the two won the right. The train left the noisy station and then after heaving a sigh of relief raced into the night. Just as Neelima was about to fall asleep, the older aunt suddenly gave a choked, frightened whisper. 'Someone is hiding here. I can hear singing. It is a trick to rob us.' They all sat up in their bunks and listened. A faint musical tinkling sound came from under the seat. The dolls, tucked at the bottom of the trunk, had been jolted all of a sudden, which had set their mechanism going, and as a result they had begun to chime and dance noisily. Neelima found it very funny, but the look of horror on all the other faces made her bow her head and keep quiet.

They reached Khulna after a sleepless night and just managed to catch the steamer which was to ferry them across the river Rupsha. Neelima had never before seen a river this wide. The muddy, pale-brown waters stretched as far as she could see, and when they had chugged their way to the middle of the river, it seemed to her that there was no land left around her any more. It took them one hour to cross the river and all the time the younger aunt kept a wary eye on Neelima, in case she sprang any more unpleasant surprises on them. She repeatedly told her to cover her face, but Neelima wanted to see everything around her, so she pretended not to hear her. Soon she actually stopped listening to the voices around her and forgot where she was. She gazed at the endless expanse of water and wondered how far the sea was. What if their steamer lost its way and swept into the sea? she thought in her usual morbid way and leaned forward so much to catch a glimpse of the sea, that she almost fell into the water. 'Tell her to sit quietly,' ordered the elder aunt and Debashish had to whisper a stern warning to his young bride, much against his wishes. He tried to teach her about the sea but Neelima just turned her face away.

By the time they reached Jatrapur, Neelima's new sari was crumpled, her hair untidy and her face streaked with black smoke. But there was a sparkle in her eyes and she looked forward eagerly to the next part of the journey and asked endless questions about the river, but the aunts only told her to be quiet as became a new bride and cover her head. At Jatrapur, they got into a metre-gauge train which was to take them across the land to another river. As they settled down once again in the small train, Neelima felt that this first journey in her life was turning out like a fairy tale adventure where the hero has to cross seven rivers and eight lands to find some precious, hidden treasure. The train moved slowly, and the landscape was now a soothing, unbroken emerald green of paddy fields. Hundreds of coconut trees stood like a wall right beside the railway tracks. Neelima could sometimes catch a glimpse of a village house and then it would be hidden again by the dense coconut groves. She saw a woman chasing a young girl, and as the train left them behind, Neelima saw the woman catch the girl's long plait and pull. She began feeling homesick and wished her mother and her own aunts were with her, instead of this disapproving group which kept telling her to cover her face and sit quietly.

The train stopped at Monihat and then the party, now all as dishevelled as Neelima, but lacking her energy and enthusiasm, got down at the small station. They walked wearily to the riverside and, after a half-hearted token bargaining, hired two boats to take them to their final destination—Bishtupur. This new river was a narrow, snake-like line of green water and covered with flowers. Neelima ran towards it and the aunts were too tired to reprimand her. She was the first one to step jauntily into the narrow boat, making it tilt dangerously to one side. She sat down heavily right in the middle. The other passengers got in, and though the boat had only enough place for six, ten people and one goat got into it. The boatman eyed Neelima, spat out betel nut juice and said, 'The bride is too heavy. The rest of you move to the opposite side of her.' This remark had an instant sobering effect on Neelima and she lost all her earlier high spirits. She now sat alone on one side of the boat and watched the boatman sullenly.

The river was thickly covered with a carpet of water hyacinths and the boatman had to push his way through the water. They wavered and lurched forward inch by inch and Neelima could hear the boatman grunting with the effort. The water had a cool, soothing look about it and hundreds of water lilies grew in the empty space amongst the hyacinth leaves. A white bird followed the boat, noisily screeching right above their heads and sometimes it would swoop down to take a closer look at what they were carrying. It suddenly took a dive right into the boat, pecked the goat sharply on its head and then flew off. 'Where is the bundle?' asked the elder aunt. 'Take care that the bird does not carry it off,' she said worriedly, watching the bird's diving expertise. Neelima did not dare to move her head, in case the bird attacked her, and sat stiffly on the edge of the boat. She could feel her old fears coming back slowly, and to distract herself, she trailed her fingers in the water. The boatman, who had never taken his eyes off her, said, 'Do not do that, there are crocodiles in the river.' Neelima's heart and head gave such a massive lurch together that the boat rocked dangerously, as if caught in a tidal wave.

The beautiful landscape turned into a nightmare in front of her eyes and, as Neelima sat there trembling, strange shapes began to emerge in the river. A grey stump, which she had earlier taken for a log of wood, now became a crocodile's tail and started lazily floating towards their boat. She glanced nervously into the water hyacinths, and there, gleaming clearly amongst the pale-pink flowers, were hundreds of hooded, evil eyes. As the boat snaked forward, twisted grey-and-yellow faces rose out of the water and each one of them was nodding and staring glassily like the collector's wife. The bird screamed more loudly than ever and Neelima sat still, numb and frozen with fear. The aunts and her husband had no idea about the trauma she was going through and were intently listening to a passenger as he talked about boat accidents. 'Just the other day, a full-grown man was dragged out from the boat near Bishtupur by a crocodile. They found his spectacles five days later near a village far down the river,' said the passenger who was a frequent traveller on the river. 'The glass was not even cracked,' he added.

Just when he was about to begin another chilling tale, the boatman said, 'There is your village, young man. Better tell the new bride to cover her face. All the elders are there.' One of the aunts quickly pulled Neelima's veil over her face and was surprised at the lifeless, docile way she hung her head down. 'She has learnt modesty at last,' thought the aunt. Neelima, breathing slowly and heavily, watched the tip of the boat approach the riverbank. As soon as it was a few feet away, she took a flying leap out of the boat. The boatman shouted out a warning and all the passengers stumbled backwards as the boat tipped up. Neelima lost her foothold, and as she was falling, through her half-covered face, she saw a white figure standing before her. She threw herself forward with all her strength and with an impressive long jump, landed right in his arms. A collective sigh went up in the crowd which was waiting behind this man and then a hushed silence fell. Neelima could not see anything but she heard her aunt scream, 'Oh Ma! The new bride has touched her eldest brother-in-law.' 'What a disgrace,' cried the other aunt, and soon a babble of voices began to rise. 'Now he will have to do penance. Poor fellow, no wedding feast for him; he will have to fast for seven days at least. Is the bride lame or is she blind to have done such a shameful thing? Touch her eldest brother-in-law, whose face she is not supposed to see even.' Debashish could not lift his eyes in shame. He knew Neelima had lost her balance, but did she have to jump out so suddenly?

The bridal party walked into the village in silence. Neelima, trembling and unsteady, kept her head down. The aunts took her to a thatched hut, pushed her in and said, 'You stay here till the puja to purify your brother-in-law is over.' She thought for a brief moment of digging her heels in and refusing to go, as in the old schooldays, but the spirit had gone out of her. She lay down in one corner of the hut and began to weep quietly. After a few minutes, she felt much better and sat up eagerly looking around her. There was a small window in the hut and through it she could see the river and the scene of her recent shameful blunder. A fishing boat had just landed with a load of prawns piled as high as a hill. Neelima quickly forgot her recent unhappy experience and happily watched the fish being unloaded. 'Maybe it is for my wedding feast,' she thought with joy, the prospect of food never failing to cheer her up.

The afternoon passed slowly and Neelima kept waiting for someone to come to the hut. She felt lonely and hungry and she also wanted to go to the toilet but did not know where to go. She went out and stood near the door uncertainly, and just then two little girls went by. 'There is the new bride who fell and …' they said pointing towards her. Neelima swallowed her anger and called them to her. She whispered her need to them. After a lot of giggling, the girls agreed to take her to the toilet. They stepped out into the open sunshine and began walking, the girls ahead and Neelima stumbling behind, blinded by her veil. The path seemed never to end and Neelima began to get desperate. Every few yards or so, the girls would stop and announce to some passerby, 'We are taking the new bride to the toilet, the same one who fell and …' the worst part of the incident was left unspoken modestly by them each time.

They walked past line after line of thatched huts, each one engulfed in a dense garden of fruit trees and vegetable plants. Guavas, papayas and mangoes gleamed off the branches and the rooftops were studded with huge, pale-orange pumpkins. There were small ponds everywhere shaded by a ring of coconut palms, and Neelima saw sideways through her veil, a young boy catch a fish with just a thin stick and a piece of string. She felt hungry and thirsty and more miserable than ever as she followed the two girls blindly. Finally, after what seemed a mile, they stopped. 'There it is. Go, we shall wait for you. Do not fall again,' they tittered rudely. Neelima lifted her veil and looked. In front of her lay a large pit surrounded by a canopy of coconut palms. In the middle of the pit, two logs had been thrown like a bridge. The girls gave her a gentle push. Neelima had no choice but to go ahead. She inched her way over the logs like a novice tightrope-walker and managed somehow to keep her balance and squat. She made her way back slowly, almost falling into the pit more than once, but each time the girls caught her. 'Poor thing, she cannot see too well or walk,' they said to everyone on the way back. 'We took her to the toilet and she almost fell in.' The news spread through the village, and by the evening, everyone wanted to see the lame and blind bride Debashish had brought from the city.

Women trooped into the little hut where she had been told to stay and peered at her. Some lifted her veil and said, 'She may be lame but she is very pretty.' 'I like a new bride to be fat and healthy,' said a plump old lady, and pulled her plait to check if her hair was real. Neelima sat helplessly in one corner and let the women examine her. She thought of the giant prawns that the boat had brought in and felt much better. 'I wonder how they will cook them here. Must be with coconut.' She did not have to wait long to find out. A huge gleaming copper plate was brought in and placed before her. The same prawns she had seen earlier, now lay immersed in a thick coconut gravy. There was hilsa too, cooked in freshly ground mustard and various other delicious preparations. Neelima, hungry and thirsty after the long journey, leaned forward eagerly to reach the plate. Suddenly a grim-faced lady said, 'You people must be mad. How can the new bride eat so much? She is not a shameless glutton, is she? Take it away and get the poor girl some rice.' As Neelima watched with one eye through the veil, the plate was whisked away and a bowl of rice was quickly put in its place. She opened her mouth to protest but something stopped her. She suddenly realized this was her punishment for the morning episode. 'But I was not to blame. It was the collector's wife who had appeared in the form of a crocodile to frighten me,' she wanted to say, but kept quiet. As the tears dropped one by one in the bowl, she began to eat the rice. She could hear the prawns' heads being cracked all around her and the hilsa bones being spat out noisily, but she did not lift her head even once. She wouldn't be a new bride for ever, would she? One day she would come back a grown woman and show them all. But now all that she could think of was the long, dangerous journey home and she wished, as she had never done before, to once again be a girl safely back at school.

Aunts and Their Ailments

1965. IT WAS WELL PAST MIDNIGHT WHEN THE TRAIN FINALLY left the New Delhi station, but Meera was so wide awake and bright eyed that it seemed to her as if the day had just begun. She did not feel tired at all, despite the fact that she, along with her three aunts, had been waiting at the station for six hours now, listening to endless announcements about their delayed train. Each time the loudspeaker cackled over their heads, Meera's aunts would retaliate with sharp curses, as if it was the voice of an old enemy who was attacking them personally, picking on them in this vast sea of people. They listened carefully, craning their necks towards the speaker, and then as soon as the announcements finished, they retorted at once. 'Idiot, brainless donkey. All this fool can do is to keep croaking "the train is late" like a frog. Can't we see the train is not here? Are we blind that he has to keep telling us over and over again that the train is late?' the eldest aunt, a frail, dignified but hawk-eyed lady, would say, spitting angrily, and her younger sisters, who were slightly faded versions of her, would add their own equally vitriolic remarks. Then, behaving strictly according to the Geneva Convention, they would keep quiet for a few moments to allow their opponent to speak his lines. The fight would then start again with renewed vigour, the aunts having recovered their breath during the brief respite. This passionate tirade against the announcements had drawn around them a small crowd of curious passengers who were also waiting for the delayed train. Greatly entertained by the three ladies' battle against an unseen enemy and happy to have something to distract them while they stood for hours wearily on the platform, they greeted each new remark with raucous laughter.

Meera, who had just turned fourteen, was extremely self-conscious of the world. She stood there hanging her face down and wishing she was an ostrich so that she could bury her head in the pile of luggage. She felt acutely embarrassed by the unwanted attention her aunts were getting and was beginning to realize that travelling with them was not going to be an ordinary journey, which in any case was already strange and adventurous enough for her to begin with.

This was the first time Meera was travelling without her parents and that too to an unknown, new town. It was an odd first journey for a fourteen-year-old girl to be making, because the aunts were going to attend the funeral of a distant relative whose relationship Meera had still not been able to grasp. They had insisted on taking her along and the dubious reason given was, 'Who knows when death will come and we should have a young person with us, to take care of the luggage.' Though Meera's father was not keen to have his young daughter travelling as a companion nurse for these elderly women, whose sanity he had always doubted, Meera's mother overruled him, saying there was no harm if the girl accompanied her sisters because 'who knows (this was a favourite opening phrase of the family) some prospective boy's mother might see her at the funeral and a good match might come out of it. Only if we start looking around early will we catch a good boy', giving the old proverb a new meaning. So the girl's best clothes were packed and the aunts told to keep their eyes on her constantly. 'As if we will not,' had been their curt answer to this request. Meera's father had been waiting at the station along with them to see them safely into their coach, but after an hour or so of nervous pacing, the aunts had sent him off with a gruff, 'We can manage. We were not born yesterday, like you.' As soon as he had left, warning Meera till the last minute of the long list of dangers that awaited her, the aunts looked at his receding back and muttered, 'Thank god, he has gone. Standing there with his long face, I am sure his blood pressure has gone up to 210.' Then they began surveying their surroundings, inspecting their fellow passengers haughtily with raised eyebrows, passing a few cutting remarks about the noisy children playing near their feet and then focusing their attention on the announcer, but always keeping an eye on their mountain of luggage and counting it every two minutes, remarking to each other loudly, 'These days the station is full of thieves.' Their audience was growing larger by the minute and two hawkers had set up their stalls nearby to add to the festive air.

Meera was now beginning to worry about the journey ahead. She had always known her aunts to be a bit odd but she had never seen them through other people's eyes like this. She watched them with embarrassment and hoped desperately that they would get tired and keep quiet. 'What will they do for twenty-four hours on the train if they have already started fighting now?' she thought, chewing her lower lip nervously.

But along with the apprehension of how the aunts were going to behave, there was also a feeling of excitement and a vague sense of pride in her own new independence. 'It will be all right once the train arrives. They will settle down in their seats and go to sleep,' she said to give herself courage. But the train did not arrive and the aunts now were getting more and more fierce in their battle against the announcer. The youngest was now standing on someone's huge, black tin trunk and waving her arms about like a seasoned politician making election promises. Meera was thankful that the unfortunate man, sitting in the depths of the station building, could not hear what the aunts were saying, but their audience seemed to be enjoying themselves thoroughly. Suddenly, they heard him announce the train and the aunts, taken aback, fell silent.

The onlookers scattered away in a hurry and everyone ran to take up positions along the platform. A few confusing minutes later, the train came hissing into the station, creating panic amongst the waiting crowd. The aunts pushed everyone in sight, and Boromashi, in her excitement, caught hold of one of the girls standing nearby, thinking it was Meera. The child screamed loudly to protest and was abandoned at once with an angry rebuke. The aunts now turned their attention to their luggage, counting them in an agitated voice once again. 'Where is the black cloth bag? It has been stolen. Coolie, coolie,' cried Boromashi. The coolie who had dozed off while waiting for the train to arrive now woke up with a start as Boromashi jabbed him painfully with her walking stick. Though she was quite capable of walking normally, the old lady insisted on carrying this heavily carved, silver-topped stick, because long ago, on the Simla Mall, she had seen an aged, regal-looking Maharani strolling with a similar one. Boromashi had searched the shops till she found one equally grand but did not use it till fifteen years later when she looked suitably old and dignified as the old Maharani. Prodded painfully by the historical stick, the coolie leapt up as if he had been bitten by a snake and then stared sullenly at them, rubbing his back.

'Get up now. We do not want to miss the train because of your drunken stupor, you lazy urchin,' the aunts snarled at him even though he was almost as old as them. The train now came to a halt and stood like a dragon, breathing heavily and blowing gushes of hot air into the platform. Everyone—the passengers, the coolies, the hawkers, and even the people who had come to see their friends off–instantly threw themselves into the coaches, and Meera was terrified that she might get separated from her aunts.

But she need not have feared. The aunts moved in and formed a fortress-like barricade around her with the skill of Roman soldiers and Meera found herself moving ahead, protected from all sides by this solid human wall. The coolie was made to walk a few steps ahead and six pairs of eyes watched his every move. 'Thieves and robbers, they all are. Where is he turning now? Keep going straight, you rascal,' the aunt shouted each time the coolie, weighed down with his load, twisted his neck to get a firmer hold on the luggage. The walking stick was about to be jabbed into his neck, but he was fortunately saved when the aunts sighted the travelling ticket inspector in one corner of the platform. Still walking in formation with Meera in the middle, they steered in perfect coordination towards the man, grabbed him by the tail of his shabby coat and shook him roughly, demanding, 'Where are our seats?' The man, right now the most important figure in the station, being pleaded to and besieged by hundreds of passengers, was so surprised by this unusual and direct treatment that he immediately gave his full attention to the aunts. 'Your names, please,' he asked Boromashi. But as he waited, his pen poised over the passenger list, the old lady turned coy all of a sudden and did not answer. Meera realized that Boromashi had forgotten her own name. She too did not know what Boromashi's real name was and turned towards the other aunts, hoping they would remember.

'Banerjee, just look for Banerjee. What do you want our names for? Just to waste time,' said Boromashi, recovering quickly. The ticket inspector could not think of an answer to that and began looking for Banerjees. Fortunately for him, all the aunts' late husbands had the same last name and a trio of Banerjees, along with a minor female, was found at the bottom of the list. The inspector pointed out their compartment to them and the three of them, with the coolie ahead and the young girl in the centre, turned around and walked like a many-legged caterpillar in the direction he had pointed.

As soon as their compartment had been found and the coolie dismissed with a pittance and a long reprimand, the aunts staked their claim to the entire area like professional highwaymen. They took turns to block the doorway and would not allow the other passengers to even pass their way. When the lone fourth member of their compartment entered, she found a solid wall of three steely-eyed, white-clad ladies facing her aggressively. 'So, you are also here?' they asked her in a shrill voice, as if the poor lady had committed some grave sin instead of just looking for her legitimate seat on the train. But the newcomer was a seasoned traveller too, and did not give away an inch. As Meera watched with admiration, she elbowed the aunts aside, ordered her coolie to place her luggage under the berth and sat down firmly on her rightful seat. Then, to clinch matters further, she placed her handbag down with a heavy thump, which clearly expressed undisputed ownership. The train whistled just then, as if it was a referee of this ladies' match and began slowly moving out of the station. For some time none spoke as both parties assessed each other. Meera thought the newcomer, despite her bold and daring stand, looked quite friendly and pleasant, but she did not know what the aunts would do next. 'God, please make them go to sleep quickly,' said Meera, watching them anxiously. It seemed as if her wish had been answered, because now the aunts began loudly arguing about who was to sleep on which berth. 'You know, Bordi, my right knee is bad. If I climb up there on that shelf they call sleeping berth, I may never be able to come down again,' said the middle aunt to her elder sister, though the message was actually meant for the younger one. But she knew that the matter would be eventually decided by Boromashi, so wasting no time she appealed directly to her. 'I and the child will sleep down here. You, Neli, go to the other lower berth. Bula and this other woman,' she said pointing an accusing finger at the fourth passenger, 'can go to the top.' Before the other lady could say anything in protest, the aunts, who had been thus given the lower berths, promptly lay down and, covering their faces with their sari ends, pretended to be fast asleep immediately. The two women banished upstairs looked at each other like enemies who have suddenly discovered a common bond of friendship and helped each other up the small, awkwardly placed steps.

The lights were switched off, and in the ghostly blue glow of the night light, Meera saw Boromashi count the luggage once more and then she fell asleep. The train rattled through the darkness, whistling in a shrill lonely voice. Once or twice Meera heard her aunt fumbling under the seat to check the locks on the various trunks, but then the gentle rocking of the train lulled her to sleep once more. When she woke up in the morning, the strong sunlight streaming in through the window almost blinded her. She rubbed her eyes and quickly sat up. The aunts looked freshly bathed and, she could tell from the eager, excited look in their eyes, ready to create trouble. They ordered Meera to go and wash her face and then search for the attendant, with whom they had already started a feud at dawn. 'But do not talk to the men standing like buffaloes along the corridors,' Meera was warned. She walked unsteadily down the train, searching for the attendant, though she did not know what he looked like.

The train lurched from side to side and Meera held on to the side to maintain her balance. She could see no men along the corridor and the only one lady, in a frilled nightgown, cleared her throat noisily in the basin. Meera walked up and down the train, enjoying the respite of being away from her aunts. At the end of the train, she found a man surrounded by trays of empty teacups. This must be the attendant, she thought and, feeling like a traitor leading an innocent man to his death, asked him to follow her.

The aunts, who were in deep acrimonious discussion with the fourth passenger, stopped and looked up with irritated faces. 'Oh, the nawabsaheb has arrived at last,' said Boromashi, her eyes sparkling with glee. 'The tea you gave us in the morning was like black ditch water. There was no sugar in it, it was coal,' she added, to open what she hoped was going to be a long and satisfying argument. But the man, frail and melancholy looking, seemed indifferent to this attack and asked them in a low voice whether they wanted lunch. 'What is there for lunch?' asked Boromashi, her earlier irritation forgotten and also somewhat disarmed by the attendant's sad, other-worldly manner. 'Vegetables, dal, rice, curd and chappati,' he mumbled, gazing far away through the window. 'What about chicken?' asked the fourth lady, and the aunts froze as if they had been shot dead. 'There is chicken too, if you want,' replied the attendant, a faint look of surprise coming into his large, watery eyes. 'Bring me a chicken lunch,' said the outsider firmly and turned to face the aunts with the defiance of a soldier going into battle all alone.

The attendant took their orders and moved ahead, leaving behind a silence so great that Meera could hear his monotonous voice, asking for lunch orders, till he reached the very end of the corridor. Then Boromashi, being the eldest, opened the court martial proceedings. 'You are a widow, are you not?' she asked the fourth lady in a sweet gentle voice, as if she was making polite conversation.

'Yes, I am. My husband was a doctor in the army. He died ten years ago. I am now going to Raipur to visit my son, who is also a doctor, a pathologist,' said the lady, eager to establish at long last the camaraderie which is an essential part of all long train journeys. But Meera, her heart beating fast, knew what was coming. 'And you eat chicken? Very strange, is it not?' remarked the middle aunt from the opposite end. 'Why should it be strange?' said the lady bravely. 'Ha! Imagine, she says why should it be strange?' cackled the youngest aunt from her perch above their heads. 'What has the world come to,' said Boromashi. 'Next, widows will be wearing frocks, lipstick and high heels.' 'Maybe go dancing like memsahibs,' cried the middle aunt, rocking with unkind laughter.

Now the doctor's widow began losing some of her earlier courage and looked helplessly about her. The three aunts stopped laughing and fixed her with a cold, unflinching stare. Realizing that she was totally surrounded, she decided to keep quiet, at least for the moment.

The train was gradually slowing down and after a few minutes stopped at a small, wayside station. The long platform stood empty, except for a family of villagers and a hawker, who rushed up to their window with a basket of pakoras. They had been freshly fried and a strong aroma of mustard oil filled the compartment. The youngest aunt leaned forward to ask for permission, and after Boromashi had nodded her head, the hawker thrust a large leaf-full of glistening, brown pakoras through the window bars. He was paid half of the amount he asked for, and as the train crawled out of the abandoned junction, the aunts and Meera began to eat greedily at once. After Meera had nudged them, they picked out one small half-burnt piece and magnanimously offered it to the doctor's widow, but she inclined her head with a quiet, strongly secretive smile. She looked out of the window in deep concentration, and when the train began to gather speed, she cleared her throat and said, 'How can you eat these dirty things? God knows in which dump they have been made!' The aunts, who had by now finished all the pakoras and were busy picking up the small bits of the crisp, dark brown crumbs with their fingertips, were, for a brief second, struck dumb. They sat staring at her, their hands suspended in front of their mouths. The doctor's widow now moved in swiftly to consolidate her gains. She stuck her neck out forward, like an attacking duck, and said primly, 'My doctor husband used to say that these things are fried in animal fat, usually pigs', because that is the cheapest. One patient of his, a healthy, young man, just dropped dead one morning. They found half a seer of pakoras in his stomach when they did the post-mortem.' The aunts now sat very still and fearfully watched the empty leaf-plate flutter as if it was a lethal insect. The younger two looked at their eldest sister desperately, knowing only she could save their honour. 'If you start worrying about everything you eat, you might as well starve,' said Boromashi feebly, a faint-green pallor creeping into her cheeks as she burped, but she looked at the fourth passenger with a grudging respect.

No one spoke for a while. The sun was now high up in the sky and the train sped through a vast, never-ending brown-and-yellow landscape. The terrain was so flat that it seemed to have been ironed out by a giant roadroller. Meera thought she could see a line of trees far away, but she was not sure. They kept swaying and merging into each other in the strong light and the green of their foliage was just a hazy blur. She put her face against the window bars, squinted her eyes to try and keep the trees in sight as long as possible, but soon she began to feel dizzy and looked away. 'How did your husband die?' asked Boromashi suddenly. Meera and the younger two aunts knew at once that this was a gesture of friendship from their leader and smiled obediently at the stranger. The fourth lady, still suspicious, was torn between her desire to talk and to remain victorious and aloof. She compromised by not responding at once and let a few expectant minutes pass before she said, 'He died of haemorrhage.' The aunts, who prided themselves for their medical knowledge, had never heard of this word but they were not going to admit it. 'We had an uncle who too died of this disease. It is quite dangerous, especially if there is an epidemic,' Boromashi said and her sisters nodded wisely to cover up the lie. The fourth lady laughed, but not in an unkind way, and said, 'You cannot have an epidemic of haemorrhage. It means bleeding inside,' she explained, happy for this chance to show her superior knowledge.

'You mean he bled to death? You should have tied a bandage,' said Boromashi, trying to redeem her side.

'No, I told you it means bleeding inside the body. You cannot see the blood except when it is too late,' whispered the fourth lady, making her eyes big and solemn.

Boromashi was silent as she digested this new and interesting fact, then she stored it away for future use. She felt very kindly towards the lady and wished she had talked to her earlier. How many new illnesses we could have found out about by now, she thought with regret. As if to make up for the lost time, she smiled broadly at her and said, 'I have high blood pressure. Both my younger sisters have diabetes. My husband died of heart failure, but he also had gout.' Meera, now bored with the unchanging landscape, was paying full attention to the conversation and she felt guilty that she had nothing to contribute to this impressive list of her family's ill health.

But it seemed as if Boromashi had read her mind and said, 'This child was born in the wrong position and her mother, my youngest sister, almost died giving birth to her.'

'My son's wife also had a very difficult delivery,' replied the fourth lady, 'but nothing compared to the pain I went through when my son was born. You see, I have a very weak digestion, so I was vomiting all the time and became as yellow and thin as this stick here,' she said, pointing to Boromashi's prized possession leaning against the doorway. Meera, who could not imagine this plump, cheerful lady ever looking like Boromashi's stick, spoke for the first time and said in a rushed, breathless voice, 'We are going to my grandmother's cousin's funeral. She is dead.'

'What did she die of?' asked the fourth lady, opening a large box of sweets and passing it around. Everyone took one after some polite refusals, and as they ate, chewing and swallowing with evident enjoyment, the middle aunt said, 'We do not know what finally took her at the age of ninety-two. Must be some mysterious disease. You know how these doctors are nowadays. When they do not know the cause of death they just say old age.' The fourth lady was about to nod her head in agreement but restrained herself since she could not let her late husband's profession down. 'Hope it was not some dreaded disease. They do not like to say it in case the family gets frightened,' she said, changing the course but remaining on the same fascinating subject of ill health and diseases. 'We would have known if it was something important,' the youngest aunt said. She reached over and unpacked a small tiffin carrier. She opened the top container and held it out to the doctor's widow. 'We never buy sweets from shops. I make them at home,' she said, as the fourth lady picked up a soft, fragrant coconut barfi. The point went home, but since there was now no animosity in the air, it did not do any harm, just balanced the score out.

The train stalled and stopped for hours for no reason at all at unknown, wayside stations where no passengers got on or off and then started off again wearily with a groan and a jolt. The aunts, after hastily declaring truce, had made the doctor's wife into a close friend already. They inquired politely about her health, but before she could really get a hold on the conversation, they cut her short and began telling her, by turns, a few choice details about their own illnesses. These were just starters and the main course was to be served later with much more drama and detail. Their lunch was brought in on steel plates with a loud clatter and dumped on the seats like a slain medieval soldier in armour. The women quickly began to eat. The aunts were happy to see the doctor's widow leave her chicken untouched. They complained together about the lunch to the attendant who took out a pencil and notebook and laboriously wrote down each point. Meera could see that the women were not satisfied with this literary kind of fight and would have much preferred a few heated words. After grumbling against the railway authorities, politicians, the government and the young people today, they dozed off in a peaceful, companionable slumber.

Their gentle snores could hardly be heard as the train rattled through vast expanses so empty that Meera felt they were the only people left on this earth. Content and happy, now that the aunts were asleep, she curled far back on the seat and looked out of the window. Once in a while she reached out and took a sweet from the fourth lady's box. The train left the bleak landscape in a great hurry and then as villages began to appear, it slowed down. Soon it had lost all its earlier urgency and crawled like a tired snail through a busy, crowded wayside town. Meera saw a group of boys on bicycles trying to race the train and she laughed out loudly when they actually managed to overtake it, shouting out gleeful catcalls. She tried not to look at the children who were squatting along the railway tracks, their naked brown bottoms facing her. Behind her, the four women, now awake and refreshed, chatted on happily as if they had known each other for many years. For appearance sake, they talked briefly about their late husbands and various children and then settled down to the serious business of discussing their innumerable ailments. Each one, her eyes sparkling with joy, described in meticulous detail her symptoms, the medicines she took, and the narrow escapes she had had from fatal diseases. Boromashi just spoke quietly and everyone listened, but the younger aunts often got up to show which part of their anatomy was being discussed. Scars long faded were brought to light, bad teeth displayed with pride and even interior organs patted and pinched to show the exact spot. Various strange noises were made to demonstrate how an aunt had choked, gagged, coughed or wheezed at some crucial moment of illness.

'They had given me up as dead. I was about to die when …' Meera heard being repeated many times. There were funny stories too about how Boromashi had been mistaken for a pregnant woman and dragged off by a nurse to the delivery room. 'I told her in Hindi, "Hamara baccha nahi hota," but the nurse just nodded grimly and said, "Ho jaiga, enema le lo,"' said Boromashi, laughing. 'Even when I was fifty-five or so, people in buses would give up their seats for me, thinking I was a helpless pregnant woman. There are many advantages of having a large stomach,' she added.

The doctor's wife remembered how her husband had once absent-mindedly operated upon the patient's brother who had come with him. 'Luckily, he too had a sore appendix. In fact, the family was very grateful and told everyone in our town that my husband could foretell illness even before the patient. It made his practice flourish even better.' Going from A–Z like a medical encyclopaedia, they talked about acidity, allergies, asthma, backaches, blood pressure, boils, constipation, dandruff, gout, tapeworms and warts.

After suitable cures had been exchanged for these and their own experiences aired, the aunts fell silent as they dozed off to replenish their strength. Some more snacks were brought out when they woke up and then Boromashi began to talk about the funeral they were going to attend. As she spoke, the simple family event gradually acquired more and more importance and finally became a spectacular event as the two younger aunts joined in to add their own half-truths to the story. 'People have been invited from all over the country; even those relatives we do not talk to are coming. The arrangements have been made by the local superintendent of police. You see, my daughter-in-law's brother is married to his daughter. The best sandalwood had been bought and at least forty kilos of pure ghee will be used,' said the youngest aunt.

'Funerals are also quite an expense these days, but I would not like to skimp and save, I told my son clearly. You get the best, I will pay for it in advance. I have opened a separate bank account for this purpose and told only my lawyer,' whispered the doctor's wife and the aunts leaned forward eagerly to listen, forming a close circle like conspirators. 'After all, you never know what these young people will do. They might be tempted to take a short cut, what with all these new gadgets like crematoria, electric ovens and all that. No, only wood, ghee and a proper ceremony with two priests will do for me. I do not want anyone to say I am a miser after I am dead. In fact, I have finished half the rituals for myself along with my husband's funeral rites. It is best to do it yourself, then you can be sure of quality,' she said, raising her finger like a preacher. The aunts, spellbound with admiration, agreed, quickly planning in their minds to open similar bank accounts as soon as they reached home.

The train now gave a loud clang and lurched to a halt. Meera saw that once more they had stopped in the middle of nowhere. But suddenly a row of children popped up one by one out of the bushes and began asking for food. The aunts snapped at them but gave them some sweets and resumed their conversation as the train moved ahead slowly again, swaying like a drunk returning home. Boromashi took the stage once more after a new batch of laddoos had been passed around.

'This aunt of ours had a premonition that she was going to die, seventeen years ago,' said Boromashi, after a short pause, which she needed to swallow the laddoo. 'She told everyone about it, but, of course, nobody believed her. But I knew at once that something would go wrong with her, because, you see, I am very sensitive to any kind of ill health in anyone,' she said, and the women nodded respectfully. 'The other day, a woman in our colony, hale and hearty, was walking past. I looked at her and said to my daughter, this one was not going to last long. Sure enough, she was dead within a week,' said Boromashi, with a satisfied sigh. The doctor's wife racked her brain desperately to think of some equally shattering anecdote.

She had already told them about her husband's brush with fortune-telling.

Boromashi gracefully allowed her time and helped herself to another sweet. 'There was a case once of two women who had the same premonition of death at the same time,' said the fourth lady after some deep thought. 'But it was about each other and they both died on the same day. In fact, one of them telephoned the other and said, "Didi, take care of yourself. I had a bad dream about you." The other woman replied, "I too," and that very moment they both collapsed on either end of the telephone line,' she ended. The hushed awe that greeted this story told her that she had pulled an ace and she settled down more comfortably, knowing she could relax now for some time and reap the reward. The talk carried on; after touching briefly on recent deaths and discussing some strange old illnesses, it went on to argue homoeopathic treatment versus allopathic treatment. The women soon discovered to their delight that the many pharmaceutical brands they took were common. The fourth lady, being a doctor's wife, had a greater knowledge of medicines and even brought out free samples for them as gift, but the three aunts were experts when it came to first- and second-hand experience of various diseases. Between them they could boast of having almost every ailment and those missing from their list had been suffered by their innumerable relatives. Each one listened eagerly as the other talked and the snacks never stopped coming out from various small tins and boxes hidden under the seat.

A range of emotions swept through the compartment as hundreds of diseases, deaths, deformities and sudden fatal mishaps vied for attention along with brief mentions of favourite foods, cheap and good sari shops, and household hints. The journey of twenty-four hours passed by in a flash and even then the women had not run out of illnesses. Meera was now beginning to feel very unwell. She was sure that she had all these illnesses the aunts had been talking about. How dangerous life was? How fragile god had made the body? But the old ladies, with their alert, sparkling eyes and loud voices, looked so strong and healthy. 'Were they really so ill?' thought Meera in confusion. The aunts had finished their own case histories and had started on strange cases they had not witnessed but heard with their very own ears, when they saw to their dismay that the train was about to reach Jabalpur. Meera began to hurriedly gather the luggage but the aunts sat back, looking sad and crestfallen. They were reluctant to leave their new friend. There were so many more interesting facts to tell her. 'Once I fractured both my thumbs together when I was ten,' said the youngest aunt, suddenly remembering important accidents from her childhood. Passengers were now coming into the compartment in search of their seats but the aunts refused to budge. They hugged the doctor's wife and promised to write to her. Meera was told to note down her address as the coolies jostled out with their luggage. They finally moved, dragging their feet from the compartment, but kept looking back and calling out to their friend, warning her to be careful about her health. But as soon as they caught sight of their relatives waiting on the other end of the platform, the aunts changed their expressions to dignified, official sorrow and began walking briskly towards them. They were the eldest, hence the most important amongst the female mourners and they made sure that the relatives knew that.

Meera, feeling shy and awkward to find herself suddenly among so many new people, tried to hide behind the aunts. But she was quickly engulfed by beaming faces that suddenly turned sad and loud, excited voices calling out greetings. Someone pinched her cheeks painfully and shouted right in her ear. Above the din and confusion, she clearly heard Boromashi announce, 'I have to walk slowly, otherwise I shall catch haemorrhage.' Then the aunts, sweeping the crowds aside and looking around sharply for a fight, surged ahead to lead the way, like brave survivors of a shipwreck.

A Child Bride

AS SOON AS MINI HEARD THE TRAIN BLOW ITS WHISTLE, SHE BEGAN TO wail. The resounding, full-throated moan of the steam engine seemed to echo her own feelings perfectly and the seven-year-old girl called back in an answering, equally ear-shattering scream. The relatives standing around the young bride were taken aback by this sudden change in her mood. Just a minute or two ago, Mini was a laughing, jangling, playful bundle of red silk and gold ornaments, which they had carried into the compartment and dumped in one corner and then forgotten all about it in the frenzy of getting all their luggage onto the train. The departure of the marriage party had jolted the small, wayside junction out of its sleepiness and now, as the train was about to leave, the confusion and excitement was at its peak. Last-minute gifts were still being exchanged and currency notes, which had been flashed around the girl's head, were now pressed into her reluctant but outstretched palms.

Now all of a sudden, Mini's muted wail had disturbed the departure ceremonies, and the relatives, all men, stopped hugging each other and turned, slightly offended by the rude interruption, to placate the little girl. They patted the bundle clumsily on various places they thought was the head, and hoped it would stop making the terrible noise. When their half-hearted efforts to quieten the bride failed, they rushed off to check their own luggage, worried that something would be stolen in the confusion. Mini, not willing to be forgotten so easily, howled even louder. The relatives were now torn between showing their sympathy and guarding their bedrolls and trunks. Where were the wretched girl's relatives, they wondered, trying to conceal their irritation with broad smiles.

Fortunately for them, the girl's maid arrived just then and took charge of her bundle. The relatives, relieved, quickly rushed back to guard their luggage. Each one of them had received expensive gifts from Mini's father and was anxious to carry them home safely. The marriage party was going back satisfied and fed to their eyebrows. For the last four days they had eaten and drunk without a break and now they sat belching contentedly, remembering the delicious food they had eaten in Mini's house. 'Such rich milk, such golden butter I have never seen in my life,' said an elderly uncle as he took a pinch of digestive powder to quieten his rumbling, indignant stomach. Mini's father, a rich landowner with eighty acres of fertile land, thirty bullocks, twenty cows and two wives, had made sure that his beloved daughter, born after seven sons, would be given a wedding that people would remember for ever.

Not only had the marriage party from the big city been fed every hour like newborn babies, and given handsome presents, Mini's father had seen to it that the girl's dowry too was as impressive as the wedding. 'Let the city people know that my girl is a princess,' he had announced to his wives and piled the entire dowry together into one lot, so that everyone got the message clearly and at once. It stood now, like a tottering pillar, in the middle of the coach where Mini had been put, along with her maid, who had looked after her ever since she had been born. Three large black trunks formed the base of the tower, and the maid, a sharp-eyed, honey-tongued old woman, had been told to make sure that everyone knew they contained twenty tolas of gold, five dozen silver plates and bowls, thirty brocade saris and a hundred silk ones as gifts for the women relatives who could not attend the wedding.

The trunks were secured with two huge locks, and for some reason, were tied up together with a sturdy rope as if they were bullocks that might run astray. Around them were stacked innumerable baskets of sweets, dry fruits and nuts. Silver-covered trays of sweetmeat peeped out from the corners where the red silk cloth covering them had been displaced. In between stood three tins of pure ghee and the heady aroma from them filled the compartment, adding to the marriage party's biliousness, but also rekindling nostalgic memories of the feasts partaken. There were a few baskets of unrefined sugar too, carelessly thrown in along with one great chunk of sugar crystal. Above this nestled baskets of small, yellow-green mangoes, guavas and heavy bunches of bananas of the same colour. Two giant-sized jackfruits had been placed precariously on top of the pile and now they rolled drunkenly on the tip of the dowry tower as the train began to move. They did not fall off, however, because they were supported by three football-sized orange pumpkins. The small spaces left between were stuffed with betel nuts, stacks of betel leaves and spices.

There was hardly any room left to move in the compartment, but though there were other empty ones on the train, reserved for the marriage party, all the relatives crowded here, as if attracted by the sickly sweet smell of the dowry tower, like flies to honey. Mini's father tried to find his daughter in the confusion, but only managed to see twinkling bits of her red bridal sari. He wanted to push the boy's relatives aside and pick up his daughter in his arms, but that would not be the right thing for the bride's father to do at all. So he tried to keep his face as stern and impassive as a wealthy, important village elder's should be, but his eyes were moist with tears. He knew he could go and see his daughter every day but even then his heart was heavy with sadness. She now no longer belonged to him. He had, chanting a few incomprehensible Sanskrit words, given her away for ever. Now she belonged to these strangers and would never return home again. It is not proper to show so much affection for a girl, his wife would reprimand him often, but this thin, dark-skinned girl was dearer to him than all his handsome, six feet tall, fair sons.

The train gave a loud sigh and began to slowly move out of the station. The crowd cleared and Mini's father caught a fleeting glimpse of his daughter's small, bangle-covered hands clutching the window bars in a tight grip. Then the train gathered speed, and within minutes, it had left the small station far behind. Mini was still crying, but her heart was not in it. She let out one last sob and then began to look out of the window, eagerly. She had never been on a train before. Just when she was beginning to settle down, humming to the rhythmic sound of the wheels and enjoying the scenery that flashed past, an old man, who came to examine the dowry closely, patted her on her head and said, somewhat belatedly, 'Don't cry, child. You will be home soon.' Mini at once began to wail again as if it was required of her. The old gentleman sprang back and the uncles quickly chorused, 'Don't cry,' and looked at the maid accusingly. The old woman put her arms around Mini and, clicking her tongue sympathetically, gave her a sharp pinch. This time Mini cried out in genuine grief, but she understood the message from the maid's sharp fingers and toned down her sobs. The uncles decided they had shown enough sympathy as required by the boy's relatives and went back to playing cards with a clear conscience.

The train was now racing through paddy fields that glimmered like a green carpet in the sunshine, and Mini, her tears already dried on her face, gazed out in wonder. She had seen this train pass her village every day but it seemed so strange to be sitting inside and watching her village from the window. It was as if everything was wrong. When they had passed the village, she was confused and wondered if she would ever see the blurred, swiftly vanishing places again, or were they disappearing for ever one by one as the train surged ahead with her, leaving them behind. Mini began to feel a strange kind of ache which was not like any pain she had known before. This was not a stomach ache which she got after eating green mangoes or an earache that sometimes woke her up at night. It was a different, heavy kind of pain which she was not sure about, but it made her very unhappy. Mini turned away from the window and curled up closer to the maid's large, shapeless figure lolling by her side. She shut her eyes and her mother's face appeared suddenly in the darkness. Mini pushed her head into the maid's lap and, feeling comforted by the familiar smell of mustard oil and tobacco, she fell asleep with her thumb in her mouth.

A jabbering commotion was going around her when she woke up next and the first thing she saw was a circle of lights

that were so bright that they hurt her eyes. She quickly shut
them up again and then slowly opened one eye. There were
only women around her now and she seemed to be sitting in
a soft, silken lap. A soothing fragrance of sandalwood engulfed
her and she heard a voice say gently, 'Talk softly, you will wake
up the child.' Mini felt she was at home again and happily
dozed off once more. The last thing she heard was someone
say, 'What a dark skin.' Mini wondered who this person was,
before she drifted off to sleep in the cosy, perfumed lap again.

The loud squeak of a koel woke her up next and she quickly
sat up. Where was she, thought Mini in panic. This was not
her mother's bed. There was no koel calling outside, but a
strange thing moving round and round above her head. Mini
felt a stab of fear in her heart. She suddenly remembered how
she had got separated from her mother in a fair once and had
been found after one frighteningly long hour. Mini did what
she had done then. She raised her face towards the ceiling and
started crying loudly.

'Stop it. You will wake up your father-in-law,' whispered
the maid's voice from somewhere under the bed. Mini stopped
crying and crawled to the edge of the bed. She was relieved
to find the maid curled up on the floor like a large bundle
of clothes and quickly jumped down next to her and said,
'Renukaki, let us go home. I do not like this place.'

The old woman cackled in a low voice and pinched Mini's
cheek playfully. 'This is your home, you silly child. You have
to spend your life here, whether you like it or not.' Mini began
to sob once again and the maid quickly changed her tone.
'But your father will come to see you soon,' she cooed. 'And
when you are older, we will go back to visit your mother. She

will give you new clothes, and me too,' she said, tickling her under the chin. Mini, laughing, hugged the old woman. 'Let's play "Ikri Mikri Cham Chikri", she said and spread her thin little hands out on the floor. She kept asking questions as the maid sleepily mumbled replies. 'Why do they have so many lights? Are they blind? What is that thing on the roof? How is it moving without a pankha-wallah? Does nobody live here?' she asked, looking around the large room.

Just then the door opened and an old woman clattered halfway in and then stood breathing heavily like a steam engine. She was the tallest and fattest woman Mini had ever seen and she filled the entire doorway. Mini thought for a moment that she had got stuck in the doorway and that is why she could not come forward. But the huge figure backed a little and then burst into the room like a charging whale. She was wrapped around in a dazzling white sari from head to toe. In one hand she carried a string of beads and in the other a stout walking stick. 'So this is what they have picked for my grandson,' she thundered, filling the room with her voice and making Mini scuttle to the maid. 'Touch your grandmother's feet,' hissed the maid, but Mini was too frightened to move.

'Let me see your face, girl. Black as coal, but you have brought a lot of gold I hear. Let me see it,' she said, pointing her stick at the maid as if it was a gun. The maid stammered and replied that the trunks were in Mini's mother-in-law's room. 'So she has grabbed them already, has she? The greedy witch. You know she wants to poison me,' she said, glaring at Mini, who quickly hid her face in the maid's sari. 'She has hidden it somewhere in the house, the poison. I know. I will find it,' said the old lady and began walking unsteadily around the room. When she had reached the other end of the room, Mini peered out from her hiding place under the maid's sari end and came face to face with a young girl, not much older than herself. She too was dressed in white and her hair was as short as a boy's. She smiled at Mini and said, 'Parbati, come to me. I am your sister-in-law. My name is Prabha.' Mini wondered who Parbati was and then she remembered that she had been given a new name after her wedding. She had forgotten what it was. 'My name is Mini,' she whispered to the girl, taking care to remain hidden from the old lady's view. Dragging her walking stick noisily on the floor she was now examining each and every item in the room as if she had never seen them before. She kept muttering to herself as she moved, and after she had inspected every corner of the room, she came to the bed and gave the pillow a resounding thump and sat down on it. A few wisps of cotton flew up and clung to her closely cropped hair. She brushed them aside angrily and said, 'How much land does the father own?' The maid answered at once, as if she had been waiting for this question.

The inquisition began. Grandmother flung rapid-fire questions at the maid but she faced the barrage with adroitness and answered the lady even before she could finish speaking. 'Do the two wives fight? Does he have a mistress in another village? How much gold has he given? Did his father murder his uncle?' she barked in quick succession, watching Mini through narrow, half-closed eyes all the time. The maid countered like a seasoned warrior and did not let her side down by hesitating or faltering even once. In fact, she added a generous amount of lies to each answer, which not only multiplied Mini's father's wealth a hundred times, it also gave him a totally new personality. By the time the cross-examination ended, he had acquired hundred more acres of land, fifty extra cows, a brand new fleet of horses and an unlimited amount of gold. The maid had also bestowed the title of Rai Bahadur on him, discarded his mistress of many years, and draped the hard-drinking, pleasure-loving man in divine, saintly robes of pure white.

The maid had done her job so well and painted such a glorious image that even Grandmother was visibly impressed and her dour face broke into a grimace-like smile. She got up and hobbled up to Mini and patted her roughly on the shoulder. 'She has a fine nose,' she said as Mini tried to pull away. 'Cover her with all the gold her father has given. It will hide her skin,' she muttered, and with a loud sigh, clattered out of the room.

The girl in white ran after her, and as she passed Mini, she gave a playful tug at her plait and made a funny face by rolling her eyes upwards. Mini burst out laughing and wanted to follow her but the maid held her back. She was about to open her mouth and let out a wail of protest, but before she could, a group of women entered the room. A thin woman with a long, sad face came up to Mini and lifted her chin. 'She is really dark. I thought her colour might look better in daylight,' she said in a whining tone. Two other women came and stood by her. They all looked at Mini with a mournful expression and clicked their tongues one by one, like a group of agitated hens. Mini's lower lip began to tremble and she pushed aside the woman's hand from her face and turned away. But a soft arm covered with gold bangles caught her and pulled her back gently. As a waft of sandalwood fragrance swept around her, Mini realized this was the same lady in whose lap she had gone to sleep last night. 'Leave her alone,' Mini heard the perfumed lady say as she held her in her arms. 'What is done is done. There is no use crying over spilt milk. So what if she is dark. My son is fair enough for both of them,' she laughed and gave Mini a tight hug. 'Come, my little doll. I will bathe you and dress you up in the pretty new clothes I have made for you. Then everyone will ask, where has this princess come from? None will dare say she is dark,' her soft voice went on talking to Mini in a soothing way, but the young girl was not listening any more. She stood still, unsure of what to do, her head spinning with shock. 'Am I ugly and black?' she thought with disbelief.

This was the first time she had ever heard anyone call her dark. At home, her parents, her elder brothers and the servants always said she was the most beautiful girl on earth and her father called her princess of the fairies. Her grandmother always said that she was as pretty as a shining star. Sometimes her friends teased her and shouted *Kah Kuchkuche* when they were playing, but she knew it was a joke. But now in this strange house, where the maid said she had to live for ever, they kept calling her dark and did not like her face. Black as coal, she remembered someone had said last night. She had not known then that they had been talking about her. Mini's eyes filled with tears, but suddenly something nudged her from inside and she swallowed her tears. Why should I cry? This is a bad house. I shall run away from it, from these ugly women, and go home right now. Mini thought and her seven-year-old, stubborn mind was made up at once. She twisted herself free from her mother-in-law's arms and ran blindly towards the door.

The women gave a gasp, but were too surprised to move. By the time they recovered, Mini had run far ahead down the corridor. They decided not to chase her and settled down comfortably to question the maid instead. 'Is it true that he has four illegitimate sons?' they began, and the maid, torn between looking after her charge and being the centre of attention, stood uncertainly in the doorway, but began answering their questions.

Mini, unpursued, had reached the end of the corridor and was now sprinting down the hall. The huge rambling house had endless corridors and rooms, and she swept past them, her footsteps echoing loudly on the polished floor. She did not know the house but managed to find ways, past rooms, halls and corridors. As she ran, she began to feel happier. She sped past two old men who stared at her in surprise, their hookahs suspended in mid-air, their chess game forgotten. She jumped over a sleeping bundle and adroitly circled a group of gossiping old ladies. Servants moving about the house on errands stopped in their tracks and then quickly moved aside to avoid a collision. One unfortunate woman, a bit slow, cried out in pain as Mini went headlong into her. Some of the children lurking in various corners of the house came out and, without stopping to ask where she was heading for, joined her in the race. But Mini did not want them. She had already done three laps and she knew the house well now. She took a few misleading turns to deftly cover her tracks and disappeared into a dark, unlit corner, while the children ran ahead, shouting in excited voices. Mini began running again. She still had no idea where she wanted to go and went round and round the house, dashing from one room to another. All she knew was that there were open fields outside the house and if she found them, she would be able to reach home. But there were only rooms with locked doors in this house and Mini ran on, searching for a way out into the open. Like a sparrow desperately trying to fly out of a locked room, she crashed blindly into furniture, pillars and closed doors.

Suddenly she saw a white figure standing ahead. It was the same girl who had come to see her with the frightening old lady. Maybe she could help her get out of this house, thought Mini, and ran faster now. When she reached her, she collapsed in a crumpled heap near her feet, panting breathlessly. The older girl picked her up and said, 'Come, do you want to see a parrot's nest?' She did not ask Mini why she was running but kept chatting to her and led her to a small room nearby. Mini was trembling still, but she no longer felt angry. But her eyes suddenly filled with tears as the girl spoke to her gently. She quickly wiped them away and cleaned her running nose with the edge of her skirt, though her maid had told her not to do so while she was here. 'I will run away later,' she thought as she followed the girl. 'What is your name?' she asked, wrinkling up her nose with a loud sniff.

'My name at home was Uma, but here they call me Prabha. Look, the parrot is there now,' she said pointing to a tree outside.

They went to the window and looked out. Mini had seen hundreds of nests in her village, not only of parrots but many other birds, but she did not want to say anything, in case the other girl felt sad that she had not seen them. Mini liked her round face with short hair and for the first time she felt happy in the new house.

'Why is your hair like a boy's?' she asked her, snuggling up close to her near the window. 'Because I am a widow.' 'What is a widow?' asked Mini, staring at her, her own bright eyes full of childlike curiosity once again. 'It means your husband is dead,' said the girl, watching the parrot. 'Was he a hundred years old, then? My maid says my husband will live for a hundred years,' whispered Mini, eager to share a secret. 'No, my husband was not a hundred. He was a few years older than I. But he fell down from the roof and died, the silly fool. Grandmother told me to wear only white clothes. She cut my hair just like hers. It was very thick and long. It hurt me when they combed it. I like it better now. My head feels so light,' she said, laughing, and asked, 'Do you have many nests near your house?' Mini began telling her about her village but suddenly behind them a loud voice called out, 'Prabha, where are you? This wretched girl needs a good beating,' it mutterred, coming closer.

Mini recognized it as her grandmother-in-law's voice and suddenly remembered that she was going to run away. She fled from the room and began racing down the corridor once more. The booming voice seemed to follow her and Mini thought the fat, crooked arms, which looked like stumps of an old tree, were going to catch her any minute. Panic-stricken, she ran into a room where the door was slightly open and quickly shut it behind her. A soothing fragrance of sandalwood greeted her like an old friend and Mini knew she was in her mother-in-law's room. Mini felt safe in this large, brightly lit room and decided to stay here till the danger of Grandmother-in-law had passed. She leaned against the door and began to look around her with curiosity.

Strange objects stood mysteriously in every corner of the room, while the ceiling and walls were covered with glittering lights. Why does she need so many lights? thought Mini, as she moved forward slowly, dazed by the bright electric bulbs.

Is she blind in one eye like the maid's mother in the village? She touched a large bouquet of flowers which stood stiffly in a vase, but when she bent her head down to find out what kind of scent they had, a puff of dust rose and tickled her nose. She shook her head and went to the next table where a strange black object gleamed in the bright light. There was a small wheel at one end with a handle attached to it. A large piece of cloth and two wooden reels of thread lay nearby. Mini knew at once that this was a sewing machine. She had heard her mother talk about it and her father had said they would get one from the city. Her heart fluttering with excitement, Mini reached out and touched the handle tentatively. It gave a whine of protest but began to turn at once and the needle too started jumping up and down soundlessly. Mini took her hand away quickly but the machine continued to move and the needle carried on its agitated digging.

Suddenly an eerie sound began to clang right on top of her head as if a large hammer was being struck and Mini, frightened, covered her head with both her arms. After a few seconds, the noise stopped and she opened one eye slightly and peered. A huge wooden box with a clock in it stood behind her. Mini had seen watches in her home and her father had even given her a small, golden one for her birthday, but this one was as big as a monster.

Everything in this house was different, strange and frightening. Could she ever get back home again? Mini thought, turning away nervously from the grandfather clock. She gave a stifled scream as she suddenly caught sight of three small figures standing silently in front of her. Then she realized that it was a mirror and she was staring at her own reflection split into three. But this was not like any looking glass they had at home. This giant mirror with lights on it could only belong to a queen. Her fears forgotten, Mini laughed with joy and ran to the huge dressing table which glittered with gold-topped glass bottles, silver boxes, lace mats and brightly coloured satin ribbons. The small bulbs above the three mirrors were like yellow gleaming eyes, and in that harsh, artificial glare, Mini saw the colour of her skin for the first time. The strange feeling of sadness which had followed her from the time she had come to this house now rose again and Mini lost interest in her surroundings. She kicked the table with her foot and looked around with a dejected air. Was 'all her life' a very long time? Were there no open doors in this house? Suddenly her eye caught sight of a round glass bowl which had a furry ball in it. Is it an animal of some kind? Mini thought and picked it up gingerly with her fingers. A cloud of scented white powder flew up in the air and settled in a fine white film over her hands.

'So this is what makes them all so fair,' cried Mini aloud to herself, forgetting her earlier melancholy at once. She laughed gleefully, her eyes sparkling like a mynah's, and dug the powder puff into the glass bowl. Holding it carefully with both hands, she covered her face liberally with the fine white powder. 'I'll show them who is dark,' she muttered, her childish heart full of a strange new feeling of revenge. But when she looked up and saw three stark white faces and six black eyes gleaming back at her from the mirror, Mini gave a loud scream of horror and then began to laugh.

At once, a faint, muffled sound of giggles floated out from under the bed, frightening Mini into silence. The laughing sound became louder now and then a thin white face with a curly mop of hair appeared slowly from under the tasselled bedcover. He was trying not to laugh but his body shook in spasms as he choked back his guffaws. Mini wanted to give the boy a kick, but just then she caught sight of her own face again and burst out laughing too. This made the boy chortle even louder and both of them began laughing loudly and the boy now rolled on the ground holding his stomach.

'Who are you?' she asked after they had quietened down a little, staring with curiosity at the boy whose face was almost as white as her own powdered face right now. 'I am your husband. Don't you remember me? I came to your house for the wedding,' he said with a worried look on his cheerful face. Mini now suddenly remembered seeing his face in the crowd of relatives. She had not seen him during the wedding ceremony because she had shut her eyes all through—since the smoke from the ceremonial fire was hurting them. After that she had fallen asleep in her father's lap. 'Why have you put my mother's powder on your face? She won't like it. It comes from England only for her. But you look so funny,' he said, giggling again.

Mini did not want to answer his question, so she asked, 'Why are you hiding under the bed?' The boy's laughing face clouded over at once and he said in a low voice, 'I have lost the gold coin your father gave me at the wedding. If my father finds out, he will beat me. That is why I am hiding under my mother's bed. She will never let him beat me,' he whispered, looking even paler than before. 'What is your name?' asked Mini. 'Arjun,' he replied in a small voice. Mini began to feel very sorry for this thin boy who was treated so badly in this house, even though he was fair. Do they like nobody? she thought. 'I will give you a gold coin. There are many in my

trunks,' she said to him and patted him on his back as she had
seen her mother do to her brothers. Arjun brightened up at
once and gave her a grateful look. But when he saw her face,
he started laughing again and said, 'You look like the clown
in the circus. You know, the short one.'

'What is a circus?' asked Mini eagerly.

'You don't know what a circus is? It has tigers, bears that
can ride cycles, and dogs that jump through fire. I will take
you one day,' he said, glancing at her shyly, his ivory-white
face gleaming in the dim light. Mini stared at him suddenly in
wonder. He was the most beautiful boy she had ever seen. 'I will
never let anyone beat him or make him cry,' she resolved firmly
in her mind and began telling him about the wild animals that
appeared in their fields sometimes. He listened with wide-eyed
wonder, the magic of circus forgotten as she spoke about the
elephant that had charged into the sugar cane field one day, how
a snake had suddenly slithered out of her mother's cupboard,
how her eldest brother had shot a panther that was going to
attack their cattle. She told him about the baby squirrel her
father had caught for her, and about the hundreds of nests that
crowded the old banyan tree near the village well. She chatted
on happily as both of them hid under the bed and it pleased
her to see that Arjun was impressed by her stories.

Suddenly they heard a clattering noise and Mini cringed
with fear at once. 'Don't be frightened. It is Grandma, but she
won't be able to see us. She is too fat to bend low,' whispered
Arjun. They held their breath and watched the old lady's feet
as she walked in and began hobbling around the room. 'Trying
to kill me, the witch. My idiot of a son cannot see it. He is
blinded by her pretty face and that sickly sandalwood smell.

But I know the truth. Voices speak to me, warn me,' grumbled the old lady in a low voice as she heaved her heavy body across the room. She went to the dressing table and picked up all the bottles one by one, sniffed them and put them back, whispering, 'Jars of magic to fool my son. "She-devil".'

When she was at the far end of the room, staring out of the window and talking to herself angrily, Arjun grabbed Mini's hand and both of them scrambled out from under the bed and shot out of the room. They ran as fast as they could and quickly reached the big hall where a crowd of relatives sat around drinking tea. A teenage girl with large, rabbit-like front teeth was singing loudly in a nasal voice, but no one seemed to be listening to her, because right behind her a heated argument was going on between a woman and her husband who seemed drunk. Mini felt oddly at home when she heard the familiar querulous notes. Her parents often fought like this at night. 'You said that the last time and I believed you. My misfortune is that I have married a liar … a drunken liar,' said the woman, addressing the attentive circle of relatives. The husband sat slouching and glared at her. Suddenly without warning he got up, shouting, 'This woman is driving me mad,' and lurched towards her. Everyone leaned forward eagerly, hoping there would be a proper fight with slaps and hair pulling, maybe even bloodshed.

But all that the man did was stumble to a table nearby and drink a glass of water noisily. 'This woman is driving me mad,' he repeated in a softer voice to himself, as if practising lines for a play. In the silence that followed, the girl started singing louder than ever, but the relatives, disappointed and let down by the anticlimax, turned away to look for other amusements.

As if on cue, the grandmother-in-law appeared from behind a pillar and took centrestage. 'I have found the poison,' she said in a trembling but powerful voice. 'The witch had hidden it in the kitchen. Now we will know the truth at last. The murderess will be caught,' she said and headed majestically towards the open courtyard which lay outside the kitchen. The relatives sprang to life and followed her at once. Arjun, Mini and Uma, who had appeared quietly behind the old lady, all joined the small procession as it moved ahead, gathering strength at every room. When they reached the courtyard, Grandmother summoned all the cooks, including the new ones who had been hired for the wedding feast, to come forward and stand in a line. They were surprised but obeyed quickly, thinking that some reward was to be handed out to them by the old lady.

'Now, where is the poison? Which one of you has hidden it? Tell me, or I will put handcuffs on you,' she bellowed. The cooks stared at her in amazement, their eager smiles frozen. 'Ma, we have nothing, no poison. We have come to cook for choto babu's wedding feast. You know us, Ma. We come to cook for all feasts in your home,' they cried, their faces sweating with nervousness. Grandmother, looking years younger now, picked up her walking stick and walked along the line of cooks, tapping each one on the neck as if he was hollow and she was testing him for suspicious sounds. The cooks stared at her with fear and smiled sheepishly with relief as she struck them and moved on. Suddenly there was a commotion. 'Take off your dhoti, you wretch,' shouted Grandmother in a shrill voice.

'But, Ma, I have no poison. Believe me, I swear,' stuttered the man, clutching his throat with his hands. Grandmother ignored his pleas and jabbed her walking stick right into his stomach.

'Open this knot. I will call the Daroga and send you to jail, you son of a devil,' she screamed. The man suddenly dropped his dhoti. There was a loud sigh of horror, topped by a high-pitched note of triumph from the old lady as a dozen squashed, gleaming with ghee, freshly made sweets fell out one by one from the fold of the discarded dhoti. The culprit now stood bow-legged and hairy-chested in his gaily striped red-and-blue drawers and glared defiantly at everyone. Then he calmly folded his dhoti under his arm and walked away from the scene of the crime.

'I told you he was the thief. I could smell the pure ghee on him,' cried Grandmother in an excited voice, her search for poison forgotten by this startling discovery of a sweets thief. 'Arjun, call your father. Tell him his beloved wife has filled the house with dacoits so that they can rob and plunder,' she shouted gleefully, 'and murder me,' she added suddenly, remembering her original quest for poison.

Arjun slinked away before she could say anything more and Uma took Mini's hand and hurriedly walked into the house. Behind her Mini could hear the old lady still shouting loudly, but relatives, satisfied with the dramatic ending, now began to move back to the hall in search of some more tea and maybe a few fresh sweets they had just seen. The cooks, who had lined up so obediently earlier for their identification parade, now laughed and chatted amongst themselves in loud voices as they went back to work. Grandmother, unhappy that her moment of triumph had ended so quickly, continued to rave, but only a few crows surrounded her now and they too were busy pecking at the scattered sweets.

The day passed slowly after this event and Mini began missing her home once more. But she had abandoned the idea of running away for a while, now that she had found Arjun and Uma. For the next two days, they played together and chatted like old friends. Mini and Arjun were often dragged off to take part in various ceremonies, but they quickly escaped and came back to Uma's small room. The young girl was not allowed to be present at any of the wedding celebrations and stayed back alone in the corner room like a prisoner confined to a cell. Arjun and Mini did not understand why she was not with them, but did not question it either, accepting it as one of the many mysterious rules that the adults had imposed on them. But they hid all the sweets that were being continually offered to them and ran back to share it with Uma as soon as the ceremonies were over. They sat huddled together on her mattress on the floor and forced her to eat the stolen sweets. They made her laugh by imitating how the various relatives ate, talked or walked. There were many other children in the house who had come with their parents to the wedding feast, but Arjun, Mini and Uma ignored them, forming a close secretive trio. The maid appeared from time to time to make sure that Mini was fed properly, but then she hurried off to hold court amongst the relatives, regaling them with wild and untrue stories about their village life and collecting generous tips.

Two days passed quickly and the army of relatives ate, slept and quarrelled happily by turns, while Arjun's mother floated around the house in a cloud of sandalwood scent and tinkling ornaments. She gave endless orders to the servants, listened to titbits of gossip the relatives offered, urged them to eat more, settled arguments that flared up every minute, and arranged new matches. She kept a wary eye on her mother-in-law, who followed her like a shadow, muttering accusations in a low, humming voice. When she came across Mini and Arjun, she patted them absent-mindedly, gave them something to eat and forgot about them.

One afternoon on the third day, when the entire household was slumbering peacefully after a huge feast, Mini suddenly began to cry for her mother and wanted to go back home at once. Uma and Arjun tried to quieten her but she shut her eyes, clenched her small fists and howled louder than ever. Arjun, bewildered and his face turning pale with anxiety by this sudden change in his bride's behaviour, went off to look for the maid. Uma, thinking of ways to distract Mini, tried to show her the nest again but she refused with a loud wail. 'Come, I will show something you have never seen before. A silver bed as small as your hand.' Mini stopped crying at once and she followed the older girl as she led her to a room tucked away in a hidden corner of the house. 'But first we have to bathe and change into puja clothes,' she said.

They went into a large bathroom gleaming with brass buckets and Uma pulled out an old white sari for Mini to wear. 'But I don't know how to; Renukaki bathes me at home,' said Mini, looking helplessly at Uma. 'I will do it for you. I too did not know how to dress myself when I came here for the first time. But I had to learn,' said the older girl and helped Mini to undress. She poured two mugs of water over her head and draped the white sari around her small frame. Mini, looking like an Egyptian mummy, stood quietly not knowing how to move. Uma bathed and changed into another white sari, and the two girls, their arms around each other, leaving a trail of wet footprints, walked into the puja room. The older girl took charge at once and began clearing the old flowers and leaves and washing the tiny silver plates and glasses. Then she gently took off the gold necklaces the idols wore and kept them aside. Mini wanted to ask Uma about the silver bed but the serious, solemn look on her face stopped her. Uma was now bathing the marble figures as she had bathed Mini a short while ago. Then she put their jewellery and clothes on again. She put some fresh flowers at their feet and lit a stick of incense. 'Shut your eyes and fold your hands,' she whispered to Mini. They silently began to chant a prayer.

Mini sat still for a few seconds but then she could not resist opening her eyes. Uma was sitting with her eyes closed but tears ran down her cheeks. She was singing in a soft voice and Mini suddenly felt very sad. At home, her mother and her aunt laughed and sang loud songs when they went to the temple. They did not sit like this, silently. Uma now finished her prayers and turned to Mini. 'Now I will show you the silver bed.' She went to a small alcove in the wall and drew aside the velvet curtain. Mini saw four tiny silver beds, each with a small frilled pillow and a mosquito net. Mini edged in closer and hoped that Uma would bring the jewelled figures of gods and put them to sleep as she did to her dolls at home. But to her disappointment, all Uma did was smoothen the sheets and tuck the mosquito nets in neatly. 'Come, let's go. But do pranam properly first.'

Just as the girls came out of the puja room, they heard a resounding thump and Grandmother suddenly appeared in front of them as large as a battleship with white sails aflutter. 'Oh, my god. What have you done?' she screamed, her large eyes almost bulging out of her head in rage. Uma shrank back from her but put a protective arm in front of Mini at the same time. The old lady lurched forward unsteadily and took hold of Uma's shoulders. She shook her roughly and then slapped her face, shouting, 'You devil's daughter. You have swallowed one grandson and you want the other. Why did you make her wear white, you jealous, evil witch?' Uma stood quietly like a lifeless figure and let the old lady shake her till her teeth began to rattle. Mini was not sure what was happening but she knew that she had to help Uma. Suddenly she jumped up and sank her teeth into Grandmother's bulging stomach. The old lady, startled by this unexpected attack, let go of Uma and turned around sharply. But Mini clung on like a baby monkey and would not let go. Grandmother heaved herself around, panting heavily and cursing, but she could not shake the girl off. They danced around the room clumsily, a blur of white.

Uma stared in amazement and then she suddenly ran out of the room. Mini let go of her victim and ran after the older girl. 'Go and change your clothes. I will send the maid. I forgot you are a bride,' she said and disappeared into the maze of corridors. Mini did not see her again for a long time. The maid came and took charge of her sobbing bride once more. 'I have been looking for you,' she cried, smiling sweetly. 'Don't cry, my heart, my princess. Soon your father will come and take you home.' But Mini was not crying to go home now. She was crying for Uma and all the strange frightening experiences that she had had in this house, which was now her home. She knew that they would not let her go to her real home any more and Renukaki was lying. She did not understand why she felt so angry and sad, and confused; she began crying as loudly as she could. It made her feel better at once. Suddenly she caught sight of Arjun lurking behind the curtains. 'I found the gold coin,' he whispered. 'Now my father will not beat me. See, I got this for you,' he held up a bright blue-green feather and Mini smiled through her tears. Arjun threw the feather up in the air and it floated lazily and landed right on the maid's head. The maid was busy cooing and calling out endearments to Mini and she did not notice the feather sitting jauntily on her head, like an emperor's plume. Arjun and Mini walked behind her, giggling in hushed tones. Mini forgot about Uma and laughed happily, watching her husband as he mimicked the maid's walk. It was the first of the many joyfully shared secrets of a lifetime ahead.

They found the feather under Mini's pillow when she died seventy years later. The bright-blue had faded to white but it was as perfect as it had been a lifetime ago.

R.C.'s First Holiday

I

RATHIN CHANDRA BANERJEE, ONE MORNING AFTER HE HAD finished his early morning tea, decided to take his family for a holiday. No one knows till today what made him take this sudden decision, since never in his entire sixty years had he ever felt the need to take a break from his strictly regimented life, the rules of which R.C. had laid down almost forty years ago. These laws were carved like edicts on stone and adhered to by R.C.'s family without any question or amendment. Then why this desire to break loose suddenly and go for a holiday? What mysterious thoughts had passed that fateful morning through the mind of this severe and silent man that made him take this drastic step so out of line from his strait and narrow path? Maybe it was the unending sameness of his morning routine of two cups of very light, Lipton Green Label tea with one and a half tablets of saccharine, and two Marie biscuits that made him suddenly want to leave home. Could it be the fact that he had never yet spoken directly to his fifteen-year-old daughter whose unexpected birth in the placid calm of middle age still shocked and embarrassed him? Did he suddenly want to get to know the stranger who was his wife or felt a guilty need to set his eighty-year-old mother free from a lifetime spent in a dark, secluded room before she passed away and left the house on her own? Whatever the reasons were, they forced him to change the pattern of his peaceful, strictly timetabled life and plunge into this journey which was to take them from Agra to Rishikesh via Mathura. He had first decided to take the women to Simla, but somehow, this hill station, still tainted by its old reputation of gay life during the Raj, seemed too frivolous. Hardwar, with its ancient temples, and Rishikesh, nestling by the sacred river Ganges, were a much better choice.

Of course, in no way was this holiday going to be a pleasure trip and R.C. made that clear right from the very start. It was a task, a pilgrimage, to be undertaken with strict discipline and fortitude. On the way stood a series of hurdles, evil temptations and pitfalls that they would have to overcome. It was going to be a true test of moral fibre and a challenge, because R.C. knew it would not be easy to suddenly take the women out of their safe, disciplined home and change their set routine for a strange, unheard of thing like a holiday. They had been trained to perfection by now, and for forty years the household had been running on a clearly defined, straight line from the very day he took charge of the family at the tender age of nineteen when his father suddenly passed away. The young, serious-eyed boy had managed, by working day and night, to payoff all his father's debts, get two plain-looking, overweight younger sisters married off, and recover money from all the non-paying clients of his father. Not only that, he had cut down household expenses by half, sacked most of the servants, packed off all the miscellaneous relatives hanging around the house, and changed the plumbing of their large, crumbling mansion. He had also found himself a wealthy wife with a vast amount of property and no brothers. It was difficult, but R.C. did it. His mind was razor-sharp and his will power unshakable. He had a wisdom well beyond his years. Only his youth was a handicap, so he forced himself to age overnight and cultivated a stern frown which not only made him look older but somewhat sinister too. But unfortunately, his curly black hair fell in unruly locks on his forehead and ruined his severe looks. He wished he could go grey soon or, better still, acquire a slight bald patch at the temples and thus look more respectable. But nature refused to toe his line and his hair grew as thick and abundant as a jungle. To make up for the lack of a dignified head, he took to wearing a pair of thick, heavy-rimmed spectacles, though his eyesight was quite good, and also gradually began walking with a slight stoop. People, especially his late father's friends, who tried to take advantage of this awkward, unusually quiet boy, were shocked to find that he was light years ahead of them in the game. 'But his father was such a warm-hearted, charming man, the whole town was his friend,' they would mutter as they reluctantly paid up long-forgotten debts.

R.C. took over his father's half-hearted, inefficient law practice and very soon turned it into a law firm of repute. Despite his young age, he was respected and held in awe all over the town and he made sure that he had no friends. Every time he felt kindly towards a fellow human being, he would remember his dying father's last words: 'Beware of friends, they will ruin you before any enemy.' So, like a tortoise, he retreated into a protective shell which was made up of cold discipline, and held fast together by rules and regulations. A very able and honest lawyer, R.C. rose high and was nominated a judge at the end of his career. Legend has it that he never had to use a hammer to call for order in his court, and even the accused, proved guilty, would listen to their jail sentence as quietly as schoolboys.

At home too, he ruled with an iron hand and his old mother who had a stubborn streak that cropped up and had to be controlled, his vague, dreamy wife whose mind kept wandering far out of his grasp, and his young, obedient but wild-eyed daughter, were all kept on a tight leash. Not even once did R.C. weaken or let go of the reins. It was not as if he ruled over them like a cruel despot, whipping them into shape. In fact, he was always kind, never raised his voice and was seen only for one hour in the morning every day. But the women could sense his silent, critical presence following them like a shadow all through the day and, sometimes, even at night, when it cast itself into their dreams, making them cry out apologies in whimpering tones. They were constantly aware of the sharp black line he had drawn for them and were always worried that they might cross it by mistake. But so far none of them had.

Ma often teetered over the borderline but had never yet fallen into disgrace. Protima, who lived in a world of her own, did not stray near even by mistake, and Ruma was too young to realize that such a step was possible. They were, strangely enough, quite contented, living the life R.C. had chalked out for them and had even got used to the nagging fear that he might disapprove, which sat weighed heavily on their shoulders. The women knew exactly what he did not like, though none of them had any idea about what he did like, if there existed such a thing. If the women had ever had the unlikely thought of making a list of things R.C. disliked and disapproved of, there were some that could be heavily underlined with a red pencil. Women talking or laughing loudly, un-punctuality, animals, films, music of any kind other than devotional or martial, fans and lights left forgotten, and anyone talking even in whispers when he was listening to the news on the radio. He did not like noisy children, hawkers who sold food on the roadside, and women with short hair. 'They should be whipped,' he often remarked, though none was sure whether it was the short-haired women, shouting children, or the poor hawkers he wanted punished, or all three. There were many other things which brought R.C.'s wrath out, but these were some of his favourite hates and the women had learnt to respect them.

But what R.C. abhorred above all was any change in his routine and not sticking to the daily timetable. The women were sharply aware of this and did not breathe easily till R.C. left the house each morning. They made sure that the servants strictly followed the code of conduct and never did anything a few minutes earlier or later. The servants, though they had been through the exercise for so many years, still trembled with fear in case something went wrong. Early morning tea of exactly the right hue, and temperature, at 6 a.m. sharp; *The Statesman* fresh and crisp, untouched by any hands except the printers' and the delivery man's; bath in cold water even in winter at 7:30 a.m. with Lifebuoy soap; Cantheridine oil rubbed precisely at 7:45 a.m. on his still abundant grey hair; by 8 a.m., dressed neatly in a pure-white shirt and trousers of a cut and style that had been in fashion when the Second World

War ended; prayers; and then breakfast of one egg boiled for two minutes precisely and one toast, which had to be brought in and placed on his plate the minute he sat down on his chair; a few seconds sooner or later had cost many a servant his job; and then off to the courts in the old Ambassador exactly at 8:30 a.m. The entire morning none spoke a single word because he did not like chatter. If need be, the women and servants used sign language or just kept quiet, saving what they had to say till his car had driven away. When he returned in the late evening, it was the same, but now they were allowed to speak to him, if they wanted to. Since none had ever wanted to, the evenings too were spent in total silence.

Not once did this routine change, and like a mighty ocean liner, it sailed through deaths, births, weddings, war and the independence of India. Once, even when R.C. was running a temperature of 105°F, he went about his usual routine and the only difference was that instead of going off to the office, he lay down on his bed, bathed and fully dressed like an important corpse about to be given a ceremonial burial.

And now after treading this strait, narrow and unwavering path for forty years, suddenly R.C. wanted a change. The women did not know how to react to this sudden storm in their deadly calm and steady lives. 'A holiday. What for? Are we children that we need a holiday? Has he gone mad in his old age?' hissed Ma, after making sure her son had left the house. Protima too was affected by the jolt and came out of the mysterious world she lived in to say, 'How shall we manage? There are sure to be so many unknown dangers on the way. How shall we know what he will dislike?' she murmured, looking frightened as a lost calf.

But the R.C. they knew never changed his mind, and anyway, he had no idea that the women were not falling in line as usual, since none had ever spoken to him directly for many years now. So, instructions were passed, they automatically did what they were told, and the group set off one morning from their quiet, green-shuttered, safe home in a shady avenue in Agra, to take on the world that lay beyond. An unknown land of chaos, unregulated lives, where rules could break down or, worse, just did not exist. This world had been waiting like a coiled snake for so long outside their door to engulf them, and R.C., who had protected the women from its evil influence for so many years, felt a twinge of apprehension as he stood with his flock on its threshold. But he showed no such signs to his women and, setting his Jaws even more firmly than usual, he led them, in a single file, to the waiting car, exactly at 8 a.m. as per schedule. He had meticulously planned each step and written out a lengthy timetable in his neat handwriting, which the members of the travelling group had to follow during the journey. Every item that had been packed was listed and allotted a number so that they could sit firmly in their proper places. The suitcases were stacked according to their importance—R.C.'s large black case was on top of the luggage while Ruma's small bag and the driver's worn out bag put at the bottom. Not trusting the untidy criss-crossing lines of the road maps, R.C. had drawn up his own route and it marched from Agra to Hardwar with military precision, with no wayward paths anywhere.

The luggage was packed into the car well in advance after careful scrutiny, since R.C. did not want a single unnecessary item on board. Then once the women had been placed in the back seat and the doors locked, the car left quietly and unobtrusively. None waved them goodbye. R.C. looked straight ahead, holding his head high, like a captain setting out to explore new lands, as he gripped the steering wheel. Next to him sat his old driver who had been with the family for many years and had managed to survive the casting out process when R.C. took over the reins. In fact, Basant was the only person who remembered seeing a young, smiling R.C., because now even his own mother had forgotten her son's childhood. She was now trying, in the cramped space of the back seat, to surreptitiously lift her feet and sit cross-legged. 'My legs cannot hang down like this. They will swell up and burst,' she whispered to Protima who sat gazing in wonder out of the window since she had never seen the streets of Agra before. Ruma was in the middle, sitting squashed behind her mother's indifferent back, with her grandmother's bony knees painfully jabbing her each time she moved. She stared in despair at the back of the two solid, white-collared necks in the front seat and wondered if this was the only view she would have during the journey. Each one preoccupied with depressing thoughts, they started off literally with a bang as the old car went straight into a vegetable-seller's cart standing around the corner. The man, startled, was about to yell an abuse, when he caught sight of R.C.'s well-known, hatchet face. His angry words remained hanging in the air and then he quickly turned them into a whacking cough. 'They should be whipped,' said R.C. under his breath.

After this inauspicious start, the rest of the journey went strictly according to the timetable. Driving slowly at a steady speed of 50 km per hour, they sailed along in total silence.

They stopped after everyone hour so that Ma could go to the toilet, and more important, wash her hands. The old lady had a great fear of dust and like Lady Macbeth she washed her hands after every hour. R.C., strangely enough, did not mind this fetish and, in fact, encouraged his mother by reminding her often. 'Cleanliness is godliness,' he would say gently and his mother would immediately rush off to the nearest tap. It was Ruma's duty to go get the water jug and pour the water for her grandmother. The old lady held out her thin, ivory-pale wrinkled hands shakily and carefully washed the imagined dirt from them three times. Then they got back into the car, the water jug was put in its right slot and the party moved on.

At one o'clock sharp, they stopped abruptly at a barren, dusty roadside and Basant got the tiffin carrier out. They had passed many shady trees on the road and could see a tall, spreading Shisham some way ahead, but according to the plan, the lunch stop was at one o'clock and R.C. saw no reason to change it to 12:50 p.m. or 1:10 p.m. So they stood in that unshaded, empty space between two trees, the afternoon sun right above their heads, and chewed their lunch slowly and methodically under the watchful gaze of a group of cows, relaxing under the shady trees nearby. R.C. did not like anyone eating quickly and made sure that he and his family masticated each mouthful thirty-two times exactly. Only Ma, who had no teeth, was exempt and could chew as many or as few times as she wished.

After the lunch had been thoroughly ground to pulp and swallowed, they set off once more. The old car went so smoothly and it seemed that all the bumps and potholes on the road had erased themselves as R.C. drove over them in his firm, resolute way. No one spoke, though once in a while Basant, who had travelled a lot with R.C.'s father, tried to point out a few interesting sights on the way, but he felt he was talking to an empty car and his voice faded away. They drove in total silence and, when the old lady coughed suddenly, Ruma gave a start, because it seemed like a gunshot in the funeral, solemn atmosphere of the car.

They reached Mathura and R.C. turned left and drove straight into a group of guides who were sitting by the side of the road like predator birds waiting to pounce on innocent travellers. One of them seized the opportunity and jumped right into the moving car. He landed right on Ma's lap and was promptly given a sharp kick by the old lady's thin but still strong legs. 'I will show you all the temples in Mathura for twenty rupees,' he gasped, nursing his injured back. 'Vrindavan will be fifteen rupees extra,' he added, keeping an eye out for Ma's feet from his awkward position on the floor of the back seat. R.C. stopped the car and got out. Ruma watched with bated breath. He put one arm in and dragged the poor man out by his collar. After soundly boxing his ears, he shoved him back to the waiting group of guides who watched the proceedings in hostile silence. A roar of abuses and mocking laughter went up as the car drove away.

'Who does the old man think he is—Dara Singh? I could have broken his legs if the ladies were not there,' the injured man screamed, hoping the other guides had not witnessed his humiliating skirmish with the old lady in the car.

R.C. drove into the holy town, his eyes gleaming angrily at the passing scenery, searching for any guides that might be lurking in the bushes. Meanwhile, news about this encounter had spread quickly through the small town, getting more and more exaggerated at each street corner, and by the time they reached the main thoroughfare of Mathura where the temple was, a crowd of howling urchins had gathered to welcome them. 'Dara Singh has come to Mathura,' they yelled as they jostled and fought to peer into the car. R.C. issued orders that no one should leave the car. He sat like a frozen statue and stared straight ahead. The children laughed and made faces at them through the windows but soon lost interest when they found there was no one in the car who could remotely pass off as the famous actor-wrestler, and except for a few beggars, everyone moved away. R.C. told the family to get out of the car and walk around. 'Talk to no one and keep to the left,' he said curtly. So they marched around in an orderly line, looking neither left nor right like a small but well-trained contingent of soldiers.

The Kansa-teela, the site of the legendary palace of Kansa, Potra, the shaded pond where Lord Krishna's swaddling clothes were said to have been washed, the ghats on the Yamuna river, and finally the most important temple of Mathura, Dwarakadhish, were all seen and not remarked upon. At each place, R.C. led the way, and as he approached, a stern-faced and dignified figure, people moved aside instinctively to give him the right of way. Ma walked slowly and lagged behind, wanting to talk to the priests who kept creeping up to her. They whispered about various interesting schemes which she could donate money to and guarantee herself a firm footing in heaven. But each time she even turned her face to look at a priest, R.C. was there standing like a stone wall between her and the promised paradise. 'Remember how much money father had given for the home for stray cattle, which still has not been built,' he said when the old lady stalled for too long once. Like horses with blinkers on, they walked around, and R.C., the silent guide, rushed them through, allowing no distractions. They saw all the well-known sights of Mathura in a blur and got into the car once more and headed towards Vrindavan. Suddenly Ma began talking. She told Ruma about how Krishna had played here as a child, how he used to steal butter and milk from the milkmaids and how much the people of Vrindavan loved him. She spoke with such warm affection, Ruma felt, as if her grandmother knew the child-god well and had caught him stealing butter or teasing the milkmaids herself. R.C., surprisingly for once, did not say anything, though they all knew that anyone talking while he drove was one of his more important dislikes.

As they approached Vrindavan, a dusty town full of temples, they could see hundreds of spires rise up in the sky like pine trees in a coniferous forest. Peacocks scuttled along the narrow paths, and R.C. almost drove over the tail feathers of a handsome male who was preening himself on the road. 'They should be whipped,' said Basant so loudly that even R.C. was taken aback. The late afternoon sun had turned weaker now and cast a mellow glow on the kadamba trees that stood near the river. Ruma, her head spinning with stories her grandmother had told her, suddenly thought she could hear faint notes of a flute being played far away. She whispered to her grandmother and they both listened, taking care to keep their secret from R.C., since they knew he would banish the fantasy from their minds at once. They did not spend too much time in Vrindavan, because R.C. had checked his watch and seen that they were running twenty minutes behind schedule. He also wanted to get away soon because he felt that the place was too full of love legends and tales of frolicking with the milkmaids, which did not give a proper and pious picture of Lord Krishna. 'All rubbish, poets' idle chatter,' he said, driving out of Vrindavan, faster than his usual 50 km. They were on the main highway again and Ma sat quietly once more. They stopped briefly once or twice so that Ma could wash her hands and the car reached Delhi just when the sun had set.

They were to spend the night at a cousin of Protima's and R.C. had written to him well in advance, informing him of the exact time of their arrival. Since they were twenty minutes early now, R.C. drove around the park near the house a few times and then when the time was right, stopped at the gate. The party, shaken up not so much by the long journey from Agra as by the several dizzy spins around the park, came into the house slowly and unsteadily. A loud scream greeted them as Protima's cousin Maya rushed towards her. 'Look at you, how you have grown,' she said in her high-pitched, laughing voice, and though the remark was obviously meant for Ruma, for some strange reason, grandmother nodded a smiling acknowledgement. More relatives ran towards them, shouting and crying out in hysterical screams as if they were going into war.

Ruma, bewildered and a bit frightened, stood quietly by the door. She had never known anyone to speak so loudly and anxiously watched her father's face. But he seemed to have turned into a stone and was staring at the ceiling like a blind man. The sound of voices was deafening now and a huge tray of tea was brought in a great flurry as more women and children appeared from hidden corners. The old lady's feet were touched by a never-ending line of children, while Protima was hugged, shaken like an apple tree in fruit, and Ruma, pinched and exclaimed over. Basant too was greeted like a long-lost friend and rushed off to the kitchen. But R.C. stood as forlorn as an island amidst this boisterous, screeching, squealing crowd. He had assessed the situation and knew it was beyond his range of control; so he quietly sat down to read the papers. He looked up periodically to catch his mother's, daughter's or wife's eye, but they, hiding within a safe circle of innumerable relatives, studiously ignored him. Once in a while someone would try to talk to R.C., and one elderly aunt even tried to joke with him, but he sat in such frozen silence that the aunt thought he was asleep and went away muttering, 'Poor man, must be tired. Not energetic like his father at all.' Soon they forgot about him. But, after a noisy and late dinner which never seemed to end, R.C. decided enough was enough and took charge once again. He appeared suddenly and quietly at the head of the crowded dining table like Banquo's ghost and ordered his family to go to bed. There was a howl of protest from the Delhi relatives, but his own clan did not let him down and obediently got up to leave the table.

R.C. made sure they left the house well before dawn so that he would not have to face anyone of them again. He was sure they would talk as loudly in the morning too. Stopping in Delhi was a mistake. But these are pitfalls we have to overcome, he thought grimly. He soon felt better once they were back on the road travelling in absolute, peaceful silence. The women felt his unspoken anger and were guilty and docile once more. They knew they had touched the borderline and wondered how it had happened. Ruma tried to breathe as softly as possible and Ma did not cough even once.

II

The journey to Hardwar was uneventful except for one incident, when the car suddenly stalled and came to an abrupt halt. Basant quickly got out to check what had happened. He emerged from under the hood, red-faced and guilty when he discovered that he had forgotten to fill water in the radiator and it was now hissing in protest. This kind of lapse was unheard of. The old car had been maintained by R.C. in perfect condition and had never dared to give a day's trouble. 'It was that stop in Delhi. Even Basant was affected by the indisciplined atmosphere,' thought R.C. angrily, but since they were running late, he let the incident pass with just a piercing, stern look, accompanied by a low-voiced, 'Discipline and duty must never be forgotten.' After Basant had trudged to a farmer's tubewell by the road and got a can of water, the car moved ahead again. Then, fortunately for the guilty party, everything went strictly according to R.C.'s timetable.

As, one by one, the milestones matched his time schedule to perfection, his earlier irritation disappeared and he forgave the women and Basant their brief folly in Delhi. 'It was the bad influence of all that shouting and laughing and the strong tea they had,' he thought and bestowed, what for him was, a benign look on the group when they had stopped for the next handwashing break. But he did not know that tiny seeds of rebellion had already been planted deep inside the heart of his flock. Each one sat silently savouring the fleeting but exciting encounter with non-believers of R.C. rules. Though they had done nothing unlawful themselves except to drink a few cups of strong tea, it was a stunning revelation to see how other people could be noisy and raucous without the wrath of the heavens falling on their heads. These people talked in the morning, never heard the news, played film songs loudly and even had a dog, and still came to no harm. Ma, Ruma, and even Protima, in a vague, muddled way, mused over their life at home, but did not say anything because the brush with the outside world was too sudden and fleeting as yet. The car purred along, passing fields of green wheat where tall white birds strolled. Sometimes parrots would fly across the road, screeching in harsh notes and R.C. would give them a disapproving glance.

After six slow, silent hours, they finally reached Hardwar. Despite the blazing afternoon sun, the air was cool and a soothing breeze swept through the car as soon as they turned the first corner. R.C.'s timetable said that they were to go straight on to the ashram in Rishikesh, so they did not stop even to wash hands, though Ma had wanted to. When they passed the crowded ghats of Har ki Pauri, the old lady peered out of the window and folded her hands. She wanted very much to stop there for a moment, but was afraid to say anything. Her heart was suddenly filled with resentment when she saw a group of women bathing in the ghats. As she watched them with envious eyes, a strange, resolute look came on her lined face, and for a moment, she looked just like her son. R.C. drove on methodically and the road now curved sharply and rose higher. Tall trees shaded the way and Ruma saw the river glistening down far below. The muddy-brown water of Hardwar had changed its hue and now flowed in a blue-green line, as crystal-clear as ice. It rushed down the boulders, forming fountains of white spray and then settled into calm pools.

The ashram they were to stay in stood a little distance from the road, and after one sharp turn which knocked Ruma's head against the front seat and made her father turn around with an angry look, they came to the gates of a rundown building. R.C. switched off the engine with a contented sigh as the hands on his wristwatch merged to show 12 o'clock exactly. Ma was the first person to stumble out of the car and she marched ahead as if she knew this place well. R.C. was a bit surprised by this sudden show of independence by his mother, but since she had already disappeared into the long corridor that led into the building, he could do nothing but trot after her at an undignified pace. Ruma led her sleepy, dazed mother, and Basant followed behind them with the luggage.

There seemed to be no one about and not a sound could be heard. The entire cool, tree-shaded building appeared to be in deep, comatose sleep. R.C., having retrieved his mother, now paced impatiently up and down the long corridor, glaring at the closed doors. He wholeheartedly approved of silence but this was going too far. Ruma peered around the tomblike halls and suddenly discovered a small room tucked away in one corner which had 'Office' written in a flowery script on its door. R.C. brushed aside the curtains and strode in, a suitable reprimand ready on his lips, but the room was empty. A faded, hand-written poster declared that 'Speech is silver but silence is golden' from one wall, and an old fan, suspended shakily from the high ceiling, whirred around lazily. R.C., already agitated and extremely irritated by the situation, caught sight of the fan and flared up with rage. Like a bull faced with a red flag, he charged towards the switch, letting off an angry gush of air, and turned it off with a sharp click. As the family watched with startled eyes, the switch bounced back and the fan continued to swirl around, and in fact gained speed. R.C. brought his hands down again heavily on the broken switch and turned it off but the little plastic square returned to its original position at once and the fan carried on as before, in what now seemed to R.C. a cheeky and impertinent manner. His family was watching him closely, mouths agape, waiting to see what his next move would be. R.C. was red in the face now and a fine sweat glistened on his forehead, though the room was cool and a soft breeze came from the fan creaking disobediently above their heads.

R.C. decided to deal even more firmly with the situation now. He stepped forward and picked up a wooden ruler that was lying on the table. Moving in quickly, as if to gain advantage, he struck out sharply at the switch. But his opponent retaliated at once like a seasoned warrior and sprang back with a noisy squeak which sounded strangely like a faint chuckle. R.C., realizing that his entire life's beliefs were at stake, lifted his arm high above his head and threw the ruler at the switch, using all his strength. It missed the enemy by six inches, found a gap in the curtains and went flying out of the door.

'What … what is this?' screamed a loud, female voice from outside the room. The next minute, a tall, well-built lady with dishevelled hair and wild, staring eyes rushed into the room, holding the ruler. 'You fool, you could have killed me. Who are you? How have you come here? This is a place for respectable people, not goondas. At your age, you should be ashamed, attacking women,' she shouted in a shrill, nerve-shattering voice at R.C. who was too stunned to move. 'Could this be happening to me?' he thought, unable to do anything. Suddenly all the doors along the corridor opened and people began to emerge as if a magic spell had been broken and the building had woken up once again. The injured woman rushed out of the room and began addressing the crowd which had gathered around them. 'This madman attacked me with a huge stick. God saved me, otherwise you people would have seen my dead body on the floor,' she said, putting her hands on her throat and making a gagging sound to give a more graphic description of her unhappy experience. 'I could have died,' she repeated. The curious circle of onlookers did not seem perturbed by this information and smiled at R.C. in a friendly way.

One very old man stepped forward, looked closely at R.C.'s face and said, 'Are you Profullo Banerjee of Agra's son?' R.C. nodded, relieved and thankful for the first time for his father's immense popularity which had reached even this far. 'He was a wonderful man, so generous, gave me 500 rupees once just like that. But you do not look as handsome and healthy. You are so pale. No flesh on you at all,' said the old man, prodding R.C. with his walking stick to check his waistline. 'Why did you attack Moni? Her voice gives one a headache, but there is no need to kill her; just a scolding would have been enough,' he said, shaking a finger at R.C. as if he was a naughty schoolboy. 'Too much violence these days ... all you young men want to be film heroes ...' he added. This was like rubbing salt on R.C.'s open wounds. He, who had never even allowed the word 'cinema' to be mentioned in his presence, was now being accused of acting like a ... film hero! His head began to spin with silent fury but he was helpless to do anything. The old man now was telling everyone what a great personality R.C.'s father had been. 'But, alas, the son … Who can say what your progeny will turn out to be … It is sad but who can question god's ways?' he said, gazing up to the sky.

Just as R.C. was thinking of getting back into the car and driving non-stop to Agra, a short, cheerful-looking man came forward and said, 'Oh! Mr Banerjee, welcome. We thought you were coming tomorrow.' R.C. was now too tired and spent with emotion to explain that he had not only sent a registered letter but a telegram as well, informing them of the exact time and date of their arrival. He just clenched his jaws, swallowed his anger and silently followed the man. The women walked in behind him as usual, but suddenly they seemed more cheerful and alert. R.C. did not like the sign at all. 'A mistake … a terrible mistake. We should return home tomorrow,' he thought grimly. The man showed them their rooms, and after a few friendly remarks which got no response, and a curious look at Protima, he went off to get their lunch organized.

Ruma ran to the window and looked out. A large, rambling garden with shady jamun and mango trees and a neat patch of vegetables stretched out far, and at the end she could see the narrow line of the river again. But it had changed from green to silver and glittered like many pieces of a broken mirror. A strong wind was blowing and yellow leaves dropped from the branches, but were blown away before they could reach the ground. As she watched, the lady with whom her father had fought came out from one of the rooms and started picking up the clothes that were drying on the ground. Then a sudden gust came out of nowhere, swirling up the dust and dried leaves into a whirlwind. It snatched the clothes up and blew them straight into the air. The lady now ran frenetically after them, hitting out wildly, but the clothes eluded her grasp each time and sailed away. She screamed a loud abuse to the skies, shaking her fist and then called out to someone inside the room. A lanky young boy came out and stood staring at her.

'You fool, don't stand there. Catch the clothes,' she shouted, still running around in circles. The boy did not move, but pondered over the problem, scratching his head. But as the lady began to approach him with an open palm, he quickly made up his mind and began chasing a bright-red blouse that was flying just past him. He lunged at it, like an agile goalkeeper, but tripped over a stone and missed the sleeve just by an inch as the blouse, billowing in the wind, rose up in the sky as if it had sprouted wings. Ruma laughed out loudly and the boy turned around, looking sheepish. He grabbed the few clothes which the wind had thrown back on the ground, and ignoring the wayward blouse which now perched tantalizingly on a low branch, he ran back into the room. The lady caught sight of Ruma and came up to her. 'This wind is blowing dust like the devil. Don't come out. Also be careful of that wicked old man who came this morning. I know something bad will happen. You see, I have this gift. I can see the future, especially if some misfortune is about to fall,' she said with a smile and reached in through the window grill to give a friendly tap on Ruma's cheek.

'Who is it? Please come in,' said Ma from behind and Protima too looked up with large, brooding eyes. Since R.C., who had been given a room in the men's wing, was not there to give instructions, the women were sitting quietly. But a strange, unknown feeling of independence stirred in them and that is what gave Protima and Ma the courage to speak to a person whom R.C. definitely was not going to like. They stared shyly at the newcomer, not knowing what to say. The lady did not need any encouragement, and in any case, silence to her meant a clear invitation to talk. She settled herself comfortably against the window frame and launched forth, 'I was telling the girl to be careful. I am Moni. My husband is a contractor in Kanpur. We have a double-storied house there. From the top-floor tenants we get Rs 1,000 per month. Next year they will increase it to Rs 1,200. We come every year to Rishikesh from Kanpur. But never have I met such a goonda,' she said and stopped to catch her breath. Her large, kohl-rimmed eyes examined them and their luggage swiftly and then settled on Protima, who was lying on the bed. 'Sorrow, I can see great sorrow in your face,' she said, looking straight at her. Protima, who was just about to go back to her earlier reclining pose, now stared at Moni, her hands twitching at her sari nervously. 'What unhappiness in those lines, what suffering. I have never seen such a tragic face in my life, and let me tell you,' said Moni unnecessarily, since no one had yet spoken a word to stop her, 'I have seen thousands of terrible faces and futures. But yours is the worst,' she said, shaking her head from side to side and banging her wrist on the grill.

Protima sat up a little and a sudden flicker of interest came into her placid, expressionless face. 'Nothing good will come to you in the future and you will only bring unhappiness to all those around you. I see death and disaster and maybe a scandal too,' said the lady in a thundering voice and rattled the window grill again. Ruma could not take her eyes off her and Ma too came and stood nearer to see the speaker better. She nudged Ruma and whispered, 'Ask her if she knows when I will die.

If it is soon, then I will not buy new rubber slippers, just make these old ones last. Why waste money,' she muttered. But the lady ignored the query and carried on studying Protima's face, reading out signs of impending doom. By the time she had finished, Protima was a changed person. Her face was alive with curiosity and her eyes had lost their fish-like stare and glimmered with excitement. She even began to talk, which was very rare, because Protima spoke about once or twice a year and only to Ma or Ruma. She got up and came to the window. 'What about my daughter?' she asked.

'You, young girl, beware of evil in the air. Grandma, you must be careful of water and fire. But, sister, what can I say to you? Your life is just a path of deep sorrow. But take care that the mad old man, who attacked me in the morning in front of all of you, does not catch you too. It seems to me he is after beautiful women,' she said, lowering her tone suddenly and rolling her eyes sideways in a coy glance.

'He is my husband,' mumbled Protima, looking down at her feet. There was a sudden silence as Moni, who was about to start on another shattering and powerful prediction, let the words hang in the air. But she quickly recovered and said, 'Oh! What can a woman do. We have to make do with anything god gives us. Now look at my husband. Good for nothing, but eating and drinking. My son fails every year but will not eat pumpkin or wear a shirt that is not ironed well. Who puts up with their wiles? It is us, the poor womenfolk. I knew it when I saw your face that there is only disaster in your fate, but I did not think it could be so terrible. That lunatic, your husband!' she said, clicking her tongue sympathetically.

Just then the door opened and R.C. walked in. Once again the room filled up with a heavy silence, but this time it seemed to continue for a long time. Then Ruma looked up and saw that the large figure had disappeared from the window and only the red blouse now flashed in solitary splendour in the garden. R.C. did not show any signs, but he had heard the lady's harsh, damaging words clearly. Ruma saw that he looked very tired and not like the R.C. they knew at home. He told them to go and have their lunch. When they came back to their room again, R.C. did not give them any timetable or orders but bestowed them a sad, quiet look and walked away. Ma and Protima sat thinking for a while, but then, unused to such mental exertion, they soon fell asleep. Ruma gazed out of the window and began to feel strangely lonely, though she had never felt the lack of company before. She had never been allowed to have friends, and the girls she knew at school ignored her, since she could not understand or join their conversations about films or boys. But now she felt that she wanted desperately to talk to someone of her own age. There was no one in sight and the ashram building had again fallen into deep slumber. Ruma looked out of the window, hoping the lady would come out once more. But she seemed to have vanished or was probably busy reading messages of doom somewhere else.

A huge, spreading banyan tree, with bronze-green leaves, fluttered at the edge of the garden and it looked so beautiful that suddenly she decided to go and sit in its shade. She glanced at the two sleeping figures on the bed and then walked to the door. Her heart beating loudly, she opened it as if it was Pandora's box. She was quite sure that her father would be lying in wait for her outside, but to her relief, the corridor was empty as usual. Her legs trembled slightly, but Ruma walked out of the ashram without once looking back. Though she was only going to a tree that stood just a short distance away, Ruma knew that she had taken a great leap into the world. Never before had she gone anywhere unless her father had told her to. Even that was quite rare. Now if she vanished in thin air, he would not know. This thought gave her an unexpected feeling of happiness and she ran to the banyan tree, which now seemed to call her like a friend she had never known. Hundreds of birds chattered from its branches and two fighting squirrels suddenly flopped down at Ruma's feet. They shook themselves, and after giving her an irritated look for interrupting their quarrel, raced away to the top of the tree in a flurry of bushy tails.

Now Ruma could see the river clearly and she walked towards it quickly, without a moment's hesitation. It was so easy to be free. Why had she not tried it before? she wondered. The river was much wider than it looked from far and Ruma could see high waves rising up in the middle. She washed her face in the ice-cold water and then sat down on a rock to savour the cool breeze and her own new self. There were not many people here, but she could see two women bathing not very far away. Their shouts of laughter as they ducked in the cold water drifted down to her. Tomorrow she would bring her mother and grandmother and they could bathe here too, she thought happily to herself. Though somewhere in the back of her mind a voice told her that her father would not allow it, Ruma, exultant in her brand-new half-an-hour-old freedom, just ignored it. She dipped her hands in water and tried to catch a leaf that was floating down.

Suddenly a small pebble landed in the water and Ruma looked up. The lanky boy she had seen in the morning was sitting on a rock and morosely throwing pebbles into the river. Heady with her new courage, Ruma got up and walked up to him. 'Did you catch the blouse?' she said in a loud, laughing voice that surprised her but gave the boy such a shock that he slipped a few inches down the rock and almost landed into the river. He hurriedly lifted himself up and smiled at her in an apologetic way. Ruma felt very shy now and they both stood silently for a while, gazing at the river. Then suddenly the boy said, 'I only failed once.' Ruma did not understand at first what he meant, then she remembered his mother's words. She wanted to reassure the boy somehow but did not know what to say. 'Can your mother really see the future?' she asked, finally, after a long pause. The boy started talking in a fast voice at once, like a dam which has burst.

'I don't know. But every bad thing that happens, she seems to know in advance. My results, my father's bankruptcy, which of the buildings he has built will collapse, our sickness, her stomach pains. Any disasters waiting to happen to our neighbours. What is the use? It only makes you feel unhappy twice, both before and after the incident.' Ruma nodded her head sympathetically as he carried on, not looking at her even once. 'It would be of some use if she could predict things like winning lottery numbers or my question papers, but no, only sad, unhappy predictions seem to be her talent. But what can we do; we have to listen to her.' Ruma felt a great empathy for this boy. She had only just realized how heavy the shackles of a parent could be. They sat and talked for a long time and Ruma was surprised to see how easy it was to talk to a person, a stranger at that. She did not worry even once what R.C. would say. He seemed to have shrunk suddenly and Ruma could not even remember the rules any more.

It was dusk when they returned to the ashram and the first person Ruma saw was her father. She prepared to meet him headlong and hoped her shaking legs and dizzy head would support her through the ordeal. What had she done, after all? Just gone to the river on her own, she told herself, clasping both her hands firmly. But R.C. just walked past her blindly and Ruma was left standing alone. Feeling somewhat cheated out of a spirited performance which she was keen to tryout before her new feeling of courage disappeared, Ruma went in to find her grandmother but there was no one in the room and she began to get worried. Could the old lady and her mother have flown away like freed birds just as she had done? But where would they go? she wondered, confused and a bit frightened for their safety.

At that very moment, the old lady was biting into a large and greasy kachori which had been fried in pure ghee in front of her eyes. A thin, emaciated man in a faded orange dhoti sat and watched her eat, coaxing her from time to time to take something more. 'Eat, Ma, eat. You have given so much to the needy, now you must look after your own self too,' he said, puffing at a beedi. Ma finished eating and then took some currency notes out from a bundle tucked in her sari. 'You pay. I do not know how much these are,' she said, giving him five hundred-rupee notes. The tea-shop owner stopped stirring a large bowl of milk and stared at her. The man in orange quickly put both his hands out and waved them like a magician. The money vanished. He whispered something to the still-dazed tea-shop man and gently guided the old lady out of the shop. 'Now I will find you a quiet place on the ghat. You can sit there and throw balls of flour to the fish. For 1001 balls it will cost you only Rs 500, which you have already paid me. Bless your kind heart. Great ladies like you are born only once in a hundred years,' he said, bowing to touch her feet. Holding on to the beedi behind his ear, he cleared a place on the bridge near Har ki Pauri and soon the old lady was sitting happily by the river, surrounded by urchins and a large tin next to her. She threw the little balls of dough, each one containing a slip of paper on which 'Ram' had been written, into the river one by one. The man in orange counted loudly and an admiring crowd drifted up to watch.

The old lady had never been happier. The taste of kachori still lingered in her mouth and she burped contentedly. Her late husband used to bring her the same kind of delicious kachoris every evening in Agra but her son had stopped all that a long time ago. She had very much wanted to eat them again before she died and went to heaven where she knew there would be no such food. Now she was happy and smiled as swarms of fat-bellied fish rushed greedily to catch the balls of dough she threw in the water. She had reached 798th and was being cheered loudly by the crowd when R.C. found her. His face set in an angry snarl, he just took her arm and pulled her up to her feet. 'What are your doing here? Where is the money you took from my bag?' he said, his voice coming out in a harsh whisper.

Ma looked at him guiltily but then suddenly she heard the crowd say, 'Leave her. It is not auspicious to stop.' Ma promptly sat down and began throwing the ball once more. The man in orange had disappeared but the crowd took up his chant, '799 ... 800 ... 801,' they cried. R.C. let go of his mother's arm to push away the urchins who surrounded him, begging for money. Very soon he could not see her at all, and each time he tried to go towards her, the crowd pushed him aside and shouted, '806 ... 807 ... 808.' R.C. sat down on the steps of the ghat and watched his mother from afar. She could see him too but she shut her eyes and began to pray loudly. She knew she was safe in the crowd, and suddenly she did not care whether her son was angry or not. She had reached Har ki Pauri, bathed in the sacred river and god would take care of her from now. When all the 1001 balls of dough had finished, and the fish, overfed and heavy, had swum away sluggishly, Ma got up. R.C. was waiting for her and she allowed him to take her back to the ashram. She returned the remaining notes to him and he did not ask her how she got there or what she did with the rest of the money. But his silence did not frighten her any more. She had broken free. When they reached back, Ruma rushed up to them. 'Where did you go?' she asked, but before the old lady, brimming with confidence and happiness, could explain, R.C. spoke in a tired voice, 'Your grandmother got lost. Where is your mother?'

Ruma was taken aback. She had thought her mother, who never stepped out without her grandmother or her father, had been with them. 'How should I know?' she answered in a voice R.C. had never heard before. What was happening to all of them? This holiday had ruined and corrupted his innocent, well-behaved family for ever. His carefully nurtured life was crumbling away into bits and racing downhill as he totally lost control. R.C. suddenly felt very old and tired. But then he saw the fat lady, his enemy of the morning battle, walking up towards them and instantly a feeling of rage surged up in his heart. He felt much stronger at once. He was just debating in his mind upon the opening words of his attack when he saw Protima emerge from behind the lady's tall figure. There was a strange expression on her face and R.C. suddenly realized she was laughing. Ruma and Ma too saw her and their mouths fell open in surprise. 'I am taking her to the "Kala baba" who knows about evil spirits. Only he can save her from a man like you,' the fat lady said and swept past them. R.C. ran after his wife, but she turned around and said softly, 'Leave me alone. I am going with my destiny. I feel so happy, now that I know what bad things fate will bring me. Moni didi is so kind to me. Only she knows about my sorrow,' she mumbled and followed her guide into the darkness. Ruma and Ma ran after her, not to bring her back, but eager to share her adventure. 'But it is night already,' was the only thing R.C. could say as the women disappeared.

He was stunned by his wife's words. This was the longest conversation they had ever had in their married life. He sat down on the steps and peered into the dark evening that had swallowed his family. He silently willed his wife to return to him. He was too proud to run after her and a nagging fear told him that she would not listen to him any more. What madness had made him come for this wretched holiday? He could hear the river roar far away and it seemed to him that it was mocking at him. He got up and walked, as if hypnotized, towards the sound. The moon appeared from nowhere and hung above his head like a bright silver disc. R.C. saw the lines on it twist into a nasty, smirking face. He had never felt so broken and weak before. He walked slowly, trailing his feet in the dust. He had feared this would happen and wished he had listened to his own inner voice that had never let him down. He thought of the old days when his very footstep would make the women scamper for cover like frightened deer. How happy they were in that quiet, disciplined home where even the wall clocks did not strike loudly because he had muffled their gongs with cloth. He kept walking further away from the ashram, thinking about those golden, peaceful days of strictly followed rules, unfailing law and order.

Suddenly he saw that he had reached the river. The moonlight cast a shimmering glow on the water and R.C. felt strongly drawn towards its silvery brilliance. He slowly walked to the edge, moving stiffly like a sleepwalker. When his feet were almost in the water, he stopped. For a few minutes he let the waves flow over his shoes. Then he took off his shoes and clothes, and carefully put them on a rock. Then, dressed in his vest and knee-length, billowing underpants, he stepped quickly into the water. The icy water gave him no shock since he had always bathed in cold water and he felt strongly happy as the river engulfed him. The waves patted his back as they swept past and then gave him a sudden, playful push which almost made him lose his balance. Though it was dark and cold, R.C. only felt the soothing warmth that seemed to flow from the river. He stood there watching the moonlight play on the water, and as the waves gently rocked him, he felt all his cares slowly leaving him. He had never known peace like this before and wondered, for a moment, if he had died and become a spirit. The waves washed over him again and again. Suddenly he saw his old self being lifted out and carried away by the rushing water. He was a child once more. His father was alive, and he, a carefree boy of ten. They had gone together to fly kites by the Yamuna and his father had suddenly jumped into the river to catch an opponent's falling kite. He too had ran in following him, and they both, forgetting the kites, had bathed happily in the muddy, weed-filled water for a long time.

As the all-forgiving, soothing waters of the Ganga washed R.C.'s years away, he remembered how different life had been once. There were so many things he had dreamt of doing, but he could not recall a single one now. He thought of his family but did not feel sad any more. He was relieved that they had broken his rules, because he no longer wanted to control them. His life had been locked up for so long, and now he wanted to break free of himself. 'Tomorrow I will buy a kite,' he said and stepped out of the river as it surged ahead, taking his past along.

To Simla in a Tonga

ONE BRIGHT, WARM MORNING, SOMETIME IN 1908, ANIMA DECIDED to wash her hair on a Wednesday instead of the usual Monday. This ordinary everyday decision changed the course of her destiny and made her travel from the quiet, peaceful town of Benares to the glamorous capital of the Raj—Simla. On the fateful morning, Anima came out on the roof and began drying her long mass of hair in the sun. She stood there, tall and elegant, shaking her heavy tresses from side to side to dry them faster and began humming softly to herself. From across the terrace, hiding behind a lace curtain, a bright-eyed, handsome face watched her silently. Then, slowly like the sun's rays passing through a heavy cloud, the intense admiring glance leapt over the clothesline, pierced the discarded frame of the string bed, raced across the rooftop, and forced her to turn her head. Their eyes met and it was the first love match of the new century. Ananda knew at once that this was the girl he was going to marry and take with him to Simla. Once he had made up his mind, everything fell into place as if by heavenly accord. All the hurdles that should have been blocking such an impulsive, unorthodox match where the boy and the girl had already made up their minds to marry, even before the elders had met and discussed their horoscopes, dowry arrangements and hundreds of other details, vanished magically. The girl's father, stunned by the audacity of this forceful young man, who had come from god knows where, to ask for his daughter's hand, had no choice but to agree. He kept up a forbidding exterior, but secretly he liked the young man, and moreover he had five more daughters to marry. Anima's mother did not give in so easily and kept warning her husband that no good would come of this hurried match.

'Who is this boy? Who was his grandfather? Where is his horoscope? Why does he not want any dowry?' she asked again and again from behind the bamboo curtain when Ananda came to their house. But the wedding took place exactly on the earliest available auspicious day that fell and before the mother could gather support amongst the relatives against the boy, they were safely married by sacred, if somewhat rushed, rites. She was helpless to do anything now except cast dark and foreboding looks at the young couple who wallowed shamelessly in their new-found happiness. 'I never thought my own daughter could shame me like this,' the mother lamented to sympathetic relatives who gathered like vultures as soon as they had heard the scandalous news.

It was relief to everyone when Ananda announced that his job in Simla had been confirmed and they had to leave immediately. 'It is a bad omen, I am telling you,' sighed his mother-in-law and the relatives. Though they did not see how a well-paid job in the secretariat could be an evil sign, they agreed with her, shaking their heads in slow, gloomy half-circles as they drank their tea. The young couple left Benares quietly one evening by train and except for Anima's brother and Ananda's friend, from whose rooftop he had first seen his bride, now declared an enemy by her family, no one came to see them off at the station. Anima's mother had wept copiously when she had left home and clutched her to her bosom. 'There are tigers in Simla. This man is taking you to the wilderness to kill you,' she cried. Suddenly she thrust a small velvet bag into Anima's hands. 'Take these gold beads. But do not tell him.'

The first thing Anima did when the train left Benares was to show her husband the gold beads. 'Keep them safely, but you will never need them. I will earn enough to keep buying you as much gold as you want,' he said proudly, though at the moment he had only ten or fifteen rupees in his pocket. The other passengers in the crowded third-class compartment heard him and shook their heads in admiration. They liked the dignified handsome young man and his tall, slim wife, whose face was as beautiful as a marble statue of a goddess. They kept offering food to the young couple, along with generous advice for a life of wedded bliss. 'Be sure to cook the food he likes,' whispered one middle-aged lady in Anima's ears and turned around at once to reprimand her husband. 'I told you not to bring this big trunk. But did you listen? No. Who am I, after all?' she hissed angrily and then started talking to Anima again in a kind voice. 'Husbands are like babies, so helpless. Look at mine,' she said and once again sharply rebuked her husband for bringing the wrong trunk. The mild-looking gentleman just smiled quietly each time she scolded him and then fell asleep with his mouth open.

The train rattled on and the vast plains of north India swept past in the darkness. One by one all the passengers fell asleep, slumped against each other like one large affectionate family. Suddenly a harsh, grating voice spoke out in the silence. 'No.

No. It will not do. Beware.' Ananda sat up quickly. He thought for a moment that one of Anima's relatives had followed them surreptitiously into the train, but then he heard a deep snore and saw that a man, curled up in the upper berth, was talking in his sleep. 'No, no,' he mumbled again, carrying on his nightmare battle and turned over restlessly. Relieved, Ananda dozed off again, but Anima, slightly perturbed by this ominous warning, could not sleep. She watched her 'husband's handsome profile and his perfect nose and fine eyebrows and gradually began to feel reassured. She leaned back against the hard wooden seat and waited impatiently for Kalka to arrive. The train raced through the night, leaving a trail of black smoke which disappeared at once into the dark sky. Sometimes a burning cinder would fly out from the engine ahead and set the grass along the tracks on fire, but then the rushing train would blow it out in a second. Anima could taste the coal dust in her mouth and her eyes hurt when she blinked.

The night seemed never to end, and Anima wondered if the train had forgotten to stop at Kalka and was now hurling them to some unknown destination over the mountains. Finally, she too was overcome by the drowsy, lethargic atmosphere of the compartment and fell into deep sleep like everyone else. But she woke up much before anyone else and sat quietly, not daring to move, in case she disturbed the lady who was dozing peacefully but heavily on her shoulders. As she watched, the sky turned lighter and slowly dawn broke far away over the horizon, turning the coal dust on the bars of the window into a silvery powder. In that faded, hazy light, Anima suddenly saw a shaky line of mountains standing far away. Then after a few minutes they were in Kalka.

All the tiredness of the journey left her and Anima rushed out of the train even before Ananda could help her out. Then she stopped suddenly in her tracks and looked about her in wonder. The small station was teeming with smartly uniformed British soldiers who strutted up and down the platform calling out cheerful greetings to each other. Nearby stood frowning and important-looking officials who, in turn, were surrounded by a small army of servants, coolies and worried babus. From the first-class compartments, pale and delicate European ladies stepped out nervously, their long dresses trailing in the coal dust, and Anima suddenly felt as if she had come to a strange, new country. She had seen Europeans in Benares too, but they were just a few ragged-looking travellers, not splendid, proud creatures like these. Though they passed quite close by her, she seemed to be invisible to them and one lady with pretty blonde curls even leaned her umbrella against her briefly as she stopped to tie a ribbon on her hat and then ran ahead with mincing steps, calling out gaily to another friend. Ananda got their few belongings out and then they quickly moved on, following the crowd and found their way out from the third-class exit gate.

They stood uncertainly on the sloping road and watched the other passengers walk away briskly. Anima knew something was bothering her husband because he had suddenly lost his self-assured manner and was chewing his trim new moustache, which he had begun to grow as soon as he had got the job, in a worried, distracted way. 'There is the new train, we can go in it … but,' he left the sentence hanging in the air. Anima knew at once what the problem was. He did not have enough money for the train tickets. Should she offer to sell the gold beads or would it hurt his pride? mused Anima, afraid of taking the wrong step so early in her married life. 'We can go by tonga, but it will take much longer,' Ananda said, not looking at Anima. 'What is our hurry? The tonga will be better. The train is new, it might roll off the mountains,' said Anima, speaking very fast. They both knew that the brand-new railway line built at an enormous cost was the pride of the British government. There was no danger of it falling off the mountains, at least for the next hundred years, but they kept silent and walked towards the tonga stand outside the station.

It was drizzling gently but persistently when the tonga set off and the narrow, curving road glistened like a snake with a brand-new skin. A long line of tongas travelled together and a few bullock-carts trailed at the end of the convoy. Most of the women passengers were sitting in the covered bullock-cart but Anima had insisted on travelling in the tonga with her husband. Ananda was once again impressed by her show of independence and looked at his eighteen-year-old bride with a new respect. Though she was ten years younger than him, there was an air of maturity about her which never failed to surprise him. She had defied her parents and married him. Now she was following him to an unknown place without any murmur of protest and was calmly undertaking a difficult and maybe even dangerous journey as if she had done it all her life. Ananda felt slightly awed by her quiet strength and silent fighting spirit. He himself had been a rebel from a very young age and defied his orthodox father by learning English. Such a scandalous and shocking thing was unheard of in his family, the priests of the oldest temple in his home town for generations and also learned Sanskrit pandits.

Scholars came from all over India to have complicated texts explained and his great-grandfather had written a lengthy, highly acclaimed discourse on the grammatical forms of Sanskrit. But Ananda learnt English, and as if that was not bad enough, he even began teaching himself Urdu from books, since no maulvi could come near his house. His father, red-faced with embarrassment and humiliation, prohibited his son from reading anything but Sanskrit, and one afternoon when he caught him on the roof with Milton's *Paradise Lost,* he gave him a sound thrashing with a cane. The entire village came to see the public flogging and were impressed with the way the old man swung the cane on the boy's back. 'That will get rid of the English madness,' said Ananda's father, happy to have a chance to display his anger to the village.

That night Ananda ran away from home, taking only his English and Urdu books with him. He roamed around various cities, doing any clerical work he could find. He taught the children of wealthy families, translated manuscripts, and even worked as a prompter in a theatre company. But all the time he was studying and improving his command over English and Urdu, and finally one day, his efforts were rewarded. A senior British officer heard of his talents and gave him a job as a translator in the secretariat. From then on he rose rapidly, and today he was going up to Simla to join the Commander-in-Chief's office as a translator. He had been on his way up but had stopped in Benares to visit an old friend and then destiny had stepped in and Anima appeared on the rooftop. She sat there now behind him, eagerly watching the breathtaking, strange, new scenery that had dramatically appeared as soon as they had taken a few winding turns after Kalka.

Anima had never seen mountains before and could not imagine that trees could grow to such a height. She took a deep breath, inhaling the spicy, fresh scent that filled the air. The tonga clattered on ahead and the bells around the horse's neck jingled softly, clashing with the sharp sounds of its cantering hooves. As they climbed up, the tonga blowing its shrill, unmusical horn at every corner, the forests became more and more dense and she could only see broken patches of sunlight filtering through weakly. It was much cooler now and Anima pulled the end of the thin cotton sari she was wearing closer around her. The road seemed endless and the mountains moved further away as they climbed. The sun suddenly dropped behind a tall peak and the road now turned silver-grey in the fading light. 'We shall stop here for the night,' announced the tonga-driver, an angry-looking man with a curling beard, which flew about wildly in the breeze when the tonga moved fast. He pointed to an old, red-roofed house and then disappeared into the darkness. Ananda took charge and helped all the passengers from the other tongas and bullock-carts, up the steep, slippery path. The house had only one large hall, divided by a bamboo screen where all of them crowded in, men on one side, women and children on the other. They spread their rolls of bedding on the floor and lay down to rest their aching backs. A long wooden box stood stolidly near the doorway and the passengers eyed it suspiciously. What was in it? Was it an empty coffin or contained some late Englishman's body? each one of them wondered anxiously, but none spoke out aloud in case it tempted the evil spirit out of the box. They spent a restless and uncomfortable night, listening to the wind howl outside and watching the box nervously. Once or twice they heard faint scratching sounds and they hoped feverishly that it was a panther lurking outside and not the Englishman trying to escape from his final resting place. Only Ananda seemed to be oblivious of any ghostly presence, and in fact, sat down on the box to put his shoes on, much to the horror of the other passengers. They left the room as soon as it was light and went and sat by the roadside, gloomily watching the beautiful, dew-drenched dawn.

At last the tonga appeared and they clambered in, and soon, to their relief, they had left the coffin far behind. The horse, now fresh and rested, raced ahead at a brisk pace, its clattering hooves breaking the silence of the mountains. Silver-haired monkeys stared at them from treetops and Anima suddenly saw a bright-blue bird flash by. They passed a village where all the children rushed out to see their tonga and an old woman brought hot tea in earthenware cups for them. For two paisa, she gave them crisp pooris and a generous amount of potato curry. Then again they were back on the road, shaking and swaying as the tonga lurched around dangerous curves. Sometimes wild cats, their yellow eyes gleaming, appeared across the road and then languidly stepped back into the shadows of the forest. 'Evil spirits, these cats,' called out one lady from the bullock-cart lumbering far behind and folded her hands in prayer. A jackal suddenly sprang at them but then moved back quickly, its handsome, silvery-grey head bowed in embarrassment for mistaking them for some edible creature. For two days they travelled like this, spending the nights at small wayside village huts where they made sure no coffins waited to share the room with them. Though the women were full of chatter when they had left Kalka and exchanged minute detail of their lives at home, now they sat silently, their voice weakened by the journey and also by the innumerable quarrels that had taken place already.

Tired and weary, every bone in their body aching, they reached Simla when the sun was about to descend into the mountains. As soon as Anima caught a glimpse of the gleaming red-roofed houses set crookedly on the hillsides, the huge deodar trees with branches that drooped sadly, she felt she had come home at last. The small town looked strangely familiar, though she had never been here before and Anima knew just exactly where the road was leading to as they walked towards the Kali Bari, the local rest house for all Bengalis visiting Simla or in transit. Ananda left Anima there, and though tired after the long journey, he rushed to the office. His old efficiency was restored once more by the heavy advance on his pay, which the clerk at the office had reluctantly doled out after saying, 'Don't make a habit of it. Sahib does not like borrowers. Never even gives his pen to anyone.'

Ananda quickly found a house and moved his wife out before the priests at the temple could ask her too many questions about his family. Though she would not be able to answer them, Ananda was afraid that the beady-eyed old men would somehow manage to ferret out whose son he was and then he would not be left alone ever. Once earlier he had been caught by an old woman who had known his lineage by just looking at his face. 'You are my sister-in-law's sister's family priest's son,' she had exclaimed and fallen at his feet. Ananda did not want that to happen again. He made sure from then on to stay away from his community and was pleased when after they had settled down in their small house, Anima, though she was polite to the other women who lived nearby, kept her distance. Her neighbours, eager to welcome this beautiful young bride, and give her their protection and advice, found her aloof and uncommunicative. The matrons of Simla shook their head disapprovingly and whispered amongst themselves that she was too beautiful to make a good wife or mother. 'These kind are always trouble. Remember Ganesh's wife? She too was a beauty, as fair as a *mem*. Within six years of the wedding she had run off with her daughter's music teacher,' said the chief lady of Fagli and the others agreed, nodding with evident glee and malice. But as time went by and Anima showed no inclination of running away with anyone, they gradually became fond of this silent, graceful girl. They stopped and talked to her whenever they saw her on the road and some women even came to ask her advice on household matters, even though she was much younger than them.

Years passed by. The First World War rumbled and then became silent far away and Simla soon grew into a crowded, bustling town as more and more families moved up from Delhi and Calcutta. Each week the train would bring in new batches of pale Europeans and dusky Indians, and while the former strode in happy to be 'as cool as home' after so long, the latter stood in long queues, answering several queries before they were let into Simla. 'Name? Father's name? Where have you come from? Where will you go back to?' was barked out in quick gunshot sentences. Most travellers answered quickly without hesitation and passed the test, but some who were too startled or frightened to answer back as smartly and swiftly were made to stand aside and vetted later by higher authorities. Once they were let in, the Indian families stayed in Simla from

April to September and then moved down again with the government to spend the winter months in Delhi. Anima did not much care for their small, dark house in Delhi and waited impatiently for winter to pass so that she could come back to Simla once more. Life was never disrupted by the yearly move, since their entire world moved with them. Schools, shops, offices, servants and even friends shunted up and down the mountain road together. Anima bought groceries in Delhi but haggled and paid for them in Simla, since the same shopkeeper came up with them. Enmities and friendships too continued without any break and each way the new surroundings gave them all a fresh lease of energy. Anima and her three daughters now travelled by the toy train and the journey was no longer a never-ending weary adventure.

Ananda was happy except for one fact. Anima refused to learn English. He tried his best to persuade her to speak in this rich, wonderful tongue, for which he had abandoned his family and home, but she set her lovely lips in a stubborn line and turned away quietly. Why should I learn English? Who will I speak it to? she thought. She did not want to have anything to do with the British, who lived a totally separate life far above them in the higher peaks of Simla. Anima had often heard strange tales about them; how they had parties where men and women danced together and music came from a special, not the marching, kind of band. They went for something called picnic at Anandale and played games like children, hitting with small hammers at a wooden ball or play-acting. They rode horses, even the women, at top speed around the hillsides and pedestrians had to quickly move out of their way. Anima had once been frightened by one such rider, lost her balance, and slipped down the deep gutter. The lady had stopped to help her up but Anima had quickly hidden herself behind a large deodar tree till the lady had gone away, muttering, 'How odd … I was quite certain … did see her …' The women in Fagli got their information about the English memsahibs not from their unsportingly taciturn husbands who worked for the English sahibs, but from an old shawl-wallah who went to sell his wares to the memsahibs. He would describe, with great drama and enjoyment, each and every detail about the English ladies and their homes to his rapt audience and paint such a fantastic, unreal picture that Anima thought the man was lying. But then once when she stepped aside to allow a line of rickshaws taking English ladies to a party pass by, and saw the pink-and-white doll-like figures, dressed in clouds of lace and silk, and smelt the heady perfume that filled the path, she began to believe the shawl-wallah's tales.

Anima not only found the English people strange and alien, she was also a little frightened by them. Once Ananda's colleague, a large, friendly young man, had suddenly decided to walk home with him and had even come into the house, much to Ananda's joy. But Anima had hidden behind the kitchen door till he had left. Ananda was very disappointed and hurt but he did not say anything to his wife. It was very soon after this that the English ghost made his appearance and began to follow Anima around. The first time she sensed his presence when she was walking back one evening from the Mall. It began drizzling and Anima decided to take a short cut through the deodar trees and turned away from the main Cart Road which she usually took. The path was moist with raindrops and the dark branches drooped down heavily as if sweeping the earth.

It was so silent that Anima could hear the water dripping from the leaves and her footsteps sounded unnaturally loud to her. Anima was not a nervous person, but something in the air made her uneasy and she began to walk faster. Then, behind her, slowly and imperceptibly, came the sound of another footstep. She did not turn around but her heart began to beat loudly. She was almost running now. The footsteps seemed to come closer and suddenly a soft voice whispered, 'Edna.' Anima looked back quickly, but all she saw were the sadly drooping branches of the deodar. The path, winding around the hillside gently, was silent and empty. Must have been the breeze, she thought, and looked straight ahead. 'Edna, dearest … please come back to me,' said the voice sharply, sounding a bit peevish now.

Anima picked up the hem of her sari and ran as fast as she could, and did not stop till she had reached the main path. Suddenly she heard voices again, but to her relief they were speaking Pahari. She knew all the ghosts in Simla were English, but she felt better when she saw four stocky Pahari coolies coming down the hillside. She asked them whether they had heard the strange voice too but they shook their heads and said, 'No, but we were busy talking ourselves. Ghosts only talk to people who are alone,' and one of them added, 'Anyway there are so many ghosts in Simla now, standing at every corner, whispering away. How many can you listen to? These poor souls must be remembering their own land, that is why they cannot remain happily buried in our soil,' he explained, shaking his head sadly, as they walked away. Anima did not tell anyone about this incident, quite sure she had mistaken the voice. But it suddenly spoke to her after a gap of a few days, when she was alone at home, and then after that continued to haunt her so relentlessly every day that she got quite used to it. 'Edna … Edna, please …' it would whisper whenever she was alone. It followed her around the house as she did the chores, stood next to her while she cut vegetables, peered over her as she cooked, sighed heavily when she went to wash clothes. Anima wished it would say something more than just 'Edna, Edna' but it did not oblige her.

In a strange way, the voice made her lose her fear of the English and she began to learn how to read and write the mother tongue of the ghost. In fact, one day, she even said, 'What do you want?' sharply to the voice as soon as it began its monotone of 'Edna, Edna'. It never spoke to her again.

Years rolled by and it was 1930 now. The country was going through great upheavals as it struggled for independence, but Simla remained aloof and above it all. Anima's three daughters had grown up now and sang 'God Save the King' at school every day and spoke fluent English with their father. Ironically, all three of them looked exactly like Anima's mother, who still continued, in her single-minded way, to warn her against Ananda. The girls, plain and sullen, had the same dismal expression of impending doom on their faces and often spoke in sharp tones to Anima, as her mother used to. Whenever they walked together, Anima, slender and elegant as ever, followed by her three squat, frowning daughters, the matrons of Fagli would never fail to remark with loud, unkind laughter, 'What ugly daughters you have produced, Anima? What use all your beauty?' The girls did not take kindly to this public humiliation and refused to walk anywhere with their mother, saying, 'Why can't you be fat like everyone else's mother?'

Ananda too was now going away from her as he climbed the ladder of promotions with dizzying speed and soon became a senior officer. Anima, left alone, slowly found herself getting more and more involved with the freedom movement. She had been secretly giving money to a friend who gave shelter to freedom fighters hiding from the British authorities. She had also learnt to spin with the wheel, but only worked at night, when her family had gone to sleep. Now she read the newspapers every day and as there were many words she did not understand, she asked her daughters to explain, but they impatiently shrugged her off. Ananda, who was so keen once that she should learn English, was not enthusiastic at all any more and looked angrily at her when she asked him what Civil Disobedience meant. Anima continued to read on painstakingly and even began talking to the women of Fagli about the freedom movement taking place in the rest of the country, but most of them did not seem very interested. 'I want the country to be free, but I do not want to throw my French saris away and wear khadi,' said one matron to Anima and that ended further patriotic talk. But there was a handful of women who listened, and one old lady, with crooked, arthritic fingers, even learnt to spin from her.

One day Anima heard that Mahatma Gandhi, who had been in jail for a long time, was coming to Simla to address a public meeting. Ananda knew about it too and told her that being an officer's wife she could not attend it; but she had already made up her mind to disobey him. Taking a garland of cotton-thread reels which she had spun herself, she quietly left the house as soon as evening fell, and walked up the ridge where the incitation was going to be held. She was very excited but sad too that none from her family was with her. She had not wanted to defy her husband but she knew that in his heart he too wanted to go. Suddenly she saw the old lady she had taught to spin step out from her house and walk hurriedly towards her. 'Anima, hide your face. Otherwise our husbands will lose their jobs,' she whispered, pulling her sari over her head. Shrouded like ghosts, they reached the place of the meeting. A circle of policemen on restive horses stood like a barrier all around but they quietly slipped through and sat down. Bapu spoke in a tired, gentle voice and she could not understand most of what he said. But everyone listened with rapt attention and she saw that many had tears running down their cheeks. When he finished speaking, Anima rushed up to him to give him the garland, but before she could move, the police charged through the crowd. Anima got hold of the old lady who had lost her spectacles and then dragged her away. They trudged home wearily, their saris torn and streaked with mud, but full of happiness for having heard Mahatma Gandhi speak.

Ananda was awake, pacing up and down the gate. He turned his face away when she entered the house. They did not speak to each other for many days, but then after one week, Ananda declared truce by bringing a rose-pink chiffon-georgette sari for her. He waved it nervously in front of her as if it was a white flag of surrender. Anima's heart melted and she took the peace offering from him with a shy smile. It was many years since he had bought her anything. But then Ananda suddenly dropped the bombshell that she had to go with him to the C-in-C's party in honour of some visiting dignitary from England. Anima knew she was trapped and could not get out of it without a major battle. Her daughters shouted with excitement and even the servant looked impressed. They ran out to spread the news and the matrons of Fagli responded with envious cries at once. This was the first time that anyone they knew had been invited by the chotta latt sahib. Ananda did not see any need to explain that it was a last-minute invitation, issued because the guest list had run short of the required number of brown faces. 'There will be senior English officers and their wives, many Maharajas and princes and generals. Maybe the Viceroy himself will come,' he said, excited as a child, but Anima sat silently. What would Bapu say if he found out, she thought worriedly. But she knew she had to go to the party, now that the entire family was egging her on. Like a goat being led to slaughter, she bowed her head and meekly obeyed her husband. For the first and last time, she vowed as she tied the slippery georgette sari and covered her neck with jewels. When she stepped into the rickshaw, Ananda gasped in surprise. She looked just like an English memsahib, but a hundred times more beautiful with her black hair and flashing eyes. Even the rickshaw-wallah stared at her dumbly, though he had seen her so many times before.

When they reached the gates of the C-in-C's residence, Ananda jumped out of the rickshaw and smartly offered her his arm just the way he had seen his boss do. But Anima stared at him in surprise. 'What happened?' she whispered anxiously. 'Has a spider got into your shirt?' Ananda put his arm down sheepishly and they both walked, with hesitant steps, into the lawns of the imposing, intimidating house. As far as her eyes could see, Anima saw nothing but shimmering white figures in strange clothes, who looked as if they had stepped out of a mythological play. The men wore many medals and the women glittered with jewellery. One lady even wore a crown. Anima had seen such people when she passed the photographer's window on the Mall, but these were even more stiff and remote-looking. A small crowd of Indian ladies stood in one corner nervously as if they were about to be shot by a firing squad. None of them spoke a word of English and they were petrified that some English lady, or worse still, man, would come forward and attack them in the foreign tongue. They silently repeated the few words that their husbands had forced them to memorize and waited for the dreaded axe to fall.

But happily for them, no one approached them, and when Anima stepped into the group, she was greeted with hysterically cheerful voices. 'Come … come, Anima, stand with us. You look like a real *mem* today,' said a thin, heavily made-up lady, giving her a quick, envious glance. She was surprised and not at all happy to see Anima at such an important gathering where only the seniormost officers had been invited, and her lovely looks made matters worse. Anima stood awkwardly, staring down at her hands. A bearer with a large silver tray strolled by them and the lady lunged forward and picked up a glass. 'Arrey, Lata, are you going to drink the water here?' asked the other ladies, aghast at her rash behaviour. But Lata ignored them and recklessly took a large gulp from the glass after speaking out her husband's oft-repeated words, 'We should change with the times,' and then adding, 'Nothing wrong,' to give herself courage. But something definitely was not right because as soon as she finished the sentence, Lata suddenly gave a stifled scream and clutched her throat. Her eyes rolled upwards and she made strange, gagging noises as if she was strangling herself. 'Oh, ooooh … god. I'm dying,' she gasped. The ladies realized that she needed help but they were not sure what kind of. 'It is the wrath of gods,' whispered a lady, another senior officer's wife standing next to Anima. Lata was now panting with her mouth wide open, as if her insides were on fire as she twisted her head from side to side. Anima fanned her with her sari end, wiping her forehead, which was now a glistening mess of sweat and face powder. Anima gently guided her to a row of chairs nearby and both of them sat down.

'It was not water … it was … Oh god … what have I done,' cried Lata in a hoarse voice, breathing heavily. A strange, unpleasant smell, almost like medicine, came from her as she spoke, and Anima, repulsed, moved back quickly. 'I will get you some water,' she said, getting up. 'No, no, not water again,' screamed Lata in a hysterical voice, speaking, for some strange reason, in English. Then suddenly, 'I absolutely agree with you,' a man's voice said just behind them and a tall, heavy Englishman appeared out of the bushes. 'Never touch the stuff. Bad for one's insides, my father used to say,' he whispered, as if sharing a secret with them. His pink face was shining with good humour and friendliness as he looked at them. Anima did not know what to do and she stood still, nervously twisting her sari. Lata was sitting with her head bowed, still groaning, and the other ladies had drifted away as soon as the Englishman had appeared. Anima desperately tried to think of some English word to say to this man but all she could remember was Civil Disobedience, and before she could say anything, the man spoke again. 'I say, where is that chap with the drinks? He had this turban. Can you see him?' he asked now, peering into the crowd in a furtive way, like a man lost in a vast desert with no water in sight. His face suddenly broke into a wide smile of relief as he spotted a glimmering turban in the midst of a group of people standing not too far away from them. 'Ha, reinforcements at last. Excuse me, ladies, be back soon,' he said and moved towards the turban with long, eager strides, his hand already stretched out in happy anticipation.

Anima watched him anxiously. Somehow she felt he was heading for disaster and she wanted very much to help him. There was a loud thump as he brought his hand down heavily on the turbaned man's back. 'A whisky ... not too much water ... bad for you ... my father ...' he said but stopped abruptly when he saw that the man carried no silver tray, just a gold-topped cane in his hands. 'Harold ... His Highness, the Rajah of Sabanpur ... Your Highness ... this is ... Lord Charwin just arrived here ...' stuttered an elderly, red-faced English gentleman in an agitated voice. Anima turned away horrified, as the man, whom she now regarded as her only friend at the gathering, shouted, 'That is jolly good for you, old man, but where is the whisky?'

People had now stopped talking and the English ladies were whispering to each other, their eyes gleaming with suppressed excitement. Anima saw Ananda at last and began walking hesitantly towards him. But before she could reach him, a heavy footstep fell behind her and a voice said, 'Edna dear, wait for me.' Anima's heart stopped. She had not heard the voice for so many years and she now quickly turned around to greet it as if it were a long lost friend. Her shy smile froze as she saw a huge, fat man with many medals on his chest waddle up towards her. His head was as round and bare as a newborn baby's and a pair of large, bulging blue eyes darted about, looking out nervously for someone. 'Edna, wait,' he cried again as Anima's heart filled with disappointment. This could not be her ghost. How could this man with a toad-like face be him? Her ghost was a tall, thin, sensitive soul with a face like Lord Byron, whose picture Anima had seen once in her daughter's English book. She forgot about searching for Ananda and stared at the impostor, feeling resentful and cheated. But then out of the twinkling darkness came a tall, thin English lady, and caught hold of the man's arm. 'I wish you would not just stride off like that leaving me alone with that drunk,' she grumbled in a low tone. 'But, Edna, I was looking for you. These medals are suffocating me,' the man said and both of them disappeared into the crowd, muttering softly and irritably to each other. Anima, relieved to have her spirit restored, walked behind them, hoping she would find Ananda. She was feeling quite annoyed with him and decided to repeat the English lady's sharp words she had heard just now, when she saw him and quickly began translating them in her mind. But Ananda looked so happy when she found him surrounded by group of important-looking men, including the imposter and his wife, that she kept her anger for later. 'Let us go home now,' she whispered. But he did not hear the words and continued to listen with rapt attention as the Englishmen talked. She caught the word 'Gandhi' and at once began to listen carefully too. Her English was not good enough to understand what they were saying, but still she managed to make sense. Her heart began to beat faster and a feeling of intense rage ran through her. 'Not fit to rule … madman,' she heard, and before she knew what she was doing, she gave the man a sudden push with all her strength and ran out blindly towards the gates. She could hear a babble of voices behind her but she kept running. An arm suddenly barred her way and Anima shut her eyes tightly, waiting for a gunshot. But there was only a rustle of silk and a faint perfume drifted up to her nose. She opened her eyes and saw an elderly English lady with large brown eyes looking at her anxiously. 'Are you all right, dear? I apologize for Harold. His hands get a little frisky when he sees a beautiful woman. I am glad you gave him a good jolt of iced water. He won't forget it in a hurry,' she said, smiling kindly at Anima. Tears welled up in her eyes and she wanted to explain to this lady why she had pushed the man, but her English failed her entirely and all she could remember was the line her daughter had taught her at home, 'Thank you for your kind invitation.'

She did not speak at all during the rickshaw ride home but Ananda watched her face, made even more beautiful by the moonlight, glow with silent rage. When Anima reached home, the first thing she did was to take off her pink chiffon-georgette sari, tear it calmly and methodically into small strips and then set fire to it in the kitchen. Feeling much calmer after that, she then bathed quickly, and dressed in a cotton sari, sat down for the first time to spin in full view of her family. Her daughters watched her nervously, their eager question about the party frozen on their lips. Ananda did not come into the room where she sat but he felt her anger following him through the house, scorching him as if she had turned into a heap of burning cinders. Anima only wore handspun clothes from that day on and never went to any party again. Ananda did not ask her even when the Viceroy invited them. Then one day, many years later, Anima asked herself whether she could accompany him to a celebration. It was August 15, 1947.

Trials of a Tall Aunt

ROOPBALA'S PILGRIMAGE TO BADRINATH AT THE YOUNG AGE OF thirty-four was planned by the gods long before she came into this world. It all started when the genes of some Amazonian ancestor, lying dormant for ages, suddenly reappeared in her, making her 5'10" tall. An unusual, but not an extraordinarily great height for a woman, but it sat upon her like a deformity and ruined her life because her 5'4"-high husband hated her from the day he set eyes on her. It was not that she was hideously ugly or undesirable in any way to merit such an instantaneous hatred from the man at first sight. In fact, she was quite pleasant to look at, with delicate features, large doe-like eyes and gleaming black tresses which reached down to her knees. Her only fault, an unforgivable one in her husband's eyes, was that she stood a clear six inches taller than he. If she had been just an inch or two above his head, then things might have been not so bad. He could have told her not to stand next to him and also taught her to stoop a little when they walked together and their married life might have been different and Roopbala would have gone for a pilgrimage to Badrinath after leading a full life, at the proper age of seventy or above. But those six extra, hateful inches which made her tower above her husband, shattering his fragile ego, altered everything in Roopbala's life.

Her husband Gajanath's heart raged with anger and humiliation every time he had to lift his head to look up to her. He was sure the villagers sniggered behind their back, and once he even heard a child in the street laugh and say, 'Look, the husband is so short and the wife like a palm tree,' but when he turned around to strangle the boy there and then, there was no one. Gajanath blamed his parents for this tragedy that had ruined his standing in society and made him an object of ridicule. How could he, the biggest landowner's one and only son, a matriculate, walk out in public with this giant of a woman trailing behind him, casting her evil shadow on his head and making him look shorter than he already was? The parents knew how unhappy their beloved son was, but they were helpless to do anything now. They had married him off to Roopbala at a very young age, when the girl had been quite dainty and petite, showing no signs of the amazon she would grow up to be in the future. She was the only daughter of a very wealthy father and they were keen to clinch the match early, before some other party grabbed her.

Child marriage had been banned by the British government recently, but what did they know about problems of finding girls with good dowry for a boy who was, to put it kindly, not exactly a beauty. In fact, they said in the village that his mother had been frightened by a bull just before she gave birth to him and the dire effects of that experience showed clearly on the child's face and temperament from a very early age. Gajanath was dark-skinned, goggle-eyed and his face was set solidly on his stocky body with almost no sign of a neck. His lower jaw was always held a few inches forward, as if ready to combat any offence that he thought had come his way. His temper flared up as suddenly as a matchstick on dry grass and his touchiness was famous in the village. No one dared to even greet him in case they said something to annoy him. They remembered how once a newcomer had made an innocent, passing remark about how the mustard had flowered so well even though it was still so short and the boy had charged headlong into the man, thrown him on the ground and bit him on his arm. The man had left the village never to come back, but the boy had waited for him with an axe for one week.

The family knew there would be trouble when they went to fetch Roopbala from her parent's house after she had reached the age of puberty. They stared aghast when she gambolled into the room as tall and elegant as a giraffe, even wondering for a brief moment if the girl had been changed, but then they remembered she was their only daughter. They kept their shock and horror well hidden, recalling the huge amount of money that had been given at the time of marriage, which had been spent already many years ago, and quickly patted the willowy girl on the shoulder, since they could not reach her head. They took her back with them to the village reluctantly, and as soon as they reached home, Gajanath, who had stayed back, threw such a dramatic and shattering fit that the entire village ran out to watch him. He ranted and raved, his short body shook with spasms and he rolled his eyes till only the whites showed. He foamed at the mouth and bit anyone who tried to come near him. In fact, he looked so much like the bull at this moment that even the animal, grazing nearby, bellowed in joyful recognition. But nothing could be done now, so the father quickly hid the bride from his son and hoped things would settle down. But five years had passed since the tall bride entered their old house, banging her forehead on the low doorway, and Roopbala's husband still hated her with the same passion. In fact, his hatred for her grew stronger every day, the flames being fanned by the fact that Roopbala seemed to be still growing taller. Everyone told him this could not be possible, because she was now twenty-one years old, but Gajanath could see her adding on inches before his very own eyes. He took care never to stand next to her or walk with her anywhere. Her very presence made this short, stocky thirty-two-year-old man break into a rage which was so strong that it covered him with a deep-red flush and made the veins on his forehead stand out. The bull began to look benign and kindly compared to him now. He never spoke to his wife even once in the last five years and had never touched her. She did not understand why he repulsed her so much and tried her best to earn his affection. She learnt to cook his favourite dishes from his mother, washed his clothes, swept and cleaned his room herself, and was always alert to his movements in the house, in case he needed something, but even then all she got for her efforts was a low, angry growl or a glare from the rolling eyes each time he saw her.

Soon she realized that the only way to make him happy was to keep out of his sight, so she began hiding each time she heard his footsteps. But she still continued to look after him, constantly alert to his every demand, yet remaining unseen. It was a lonely, sad life for her in the old house and Roopbala often wondered why. She spent her time reading religious books, praying and stitching clothes for all the needy children of the village. Her mother-in-law treated her with contempt too, but since she was afraid of her husband, who was fond of Roopbala, she did not dare say anything openly. But she muttered constantly under her breath. 'God knows what they fed her at home to make her into a mountain. It is shameless for a woman to be so tall,' she would say to all the visitors and Roopbala merged further into the shadows to hide herself. The years passed slowly, filled with a never-ending, heavy gloom. Her father-in-law, who had always been kind to her and protected her from the son, passed away, and just a few months after that her mother-in-law too died, lamenting to the last that she had seen no grandchild.

Now Roopbala and Gajanath were alone in the huge, empty house. They lived in an oasis of oppressive silence, while around them trees flowered, birds sang continuously in joyful notes and the village children played noisy, cheerful games just outside their doorstep. Roopbala often watched them from the window but dared not go out to the village, because her husband hated her appearing in public. But Gajanath himself often went out at night and stayed away till early morning and Roopbala was left alone in the stifling, dark house. There had been a few old servants, but they too left one by one, unable to bear the depressing atmosphere that had now taken over the entire house. 'They are like two ghosts walking around. Chhoto babu does not see her, but hates even her shadow. Boudi just sits quietly all day. I feel scared with them. Give me a good, nagging housewife any day; at least they are real flesh and blood,' said the last surviving old maidservant after she had packed up and left.

Roopbala now did all the work by herself, and one day, when she was reaching out to pick up a jar from the highest shelf, Gajanath decided to murder her. The sight of her long arm, easily picking up things from places where he could reach only by standing on a stool, drove him blind with rage and his crazed mind began weaving schemes to get rid of this witch his parents had saddled him with. He had started drinking heavily ever since his father had died, and his eyes, bloodshot to begin with, were now two deep-crimson pools. He seemed to have shrunk with age while his once-lissom wife had grown quite heavy and now stood not only taller but more solidly built than him. 'Had she been a normal-sized woman, I could have easily strangled her. But this mountain, how will I get rid of this mountain?' he thought, trembling with anger. How much poison will she need for that body? he thought with disgust. Then, as he was going to lift his glass to his lips, he suddenly saw his father's shotgun hanging on the wall. His father had kept this loaded gun ever since a thief had crept into the house and stolen the silver spittoon from right under his bed as he slept. 'I will shoot her, the elephant,' he thought excitedly and almost spilt his glass of country liquor. 'I will shoot her with father's gun. He brought this monster home for me, his gun can get rid of her now.'

Roopbala went about doing her chores in the kitchen, unaware of the plot of her imminent murder. Like every night, she served the food in a plate, and after leaving it outside his room, she ate herself and went to sleep. Gajanath waited till the moon was high up in the sky and then he put his glass down and walked unsteadily to the wall where the gun was hanging. He stretched out his arm to take if off the nail, but the gun was hanging far above his reach. Cursing loudly, he picked up a chair and dragged it to the wall. 'Everything has been made for giants in this house,' he muttered and climbed on the chair, his legs shaking. Just as his fingers had closed on the butt of the gun, the leg of the rickety old chair collapsed under him and he fell with a thundering crash. The entire empty and silent house echoed his downfall, magnifying it tenfold and Roopbala came running into the room. 'What is it? What happened?' she said, taking care to stay out of sight. Gajanath lay sprawled on the floor, sweat was pouring down his flushed face and he wiped it angrily with his hand. Then he picked up the gun which had fallen on the floor with him. 'I am going to kill you, you shameless, tall, witch of a woman,' he slurred as he tried to get up. Roopbala moved back alarmed. Gajanath took two faltering steps forward. 'Don't. Please don't. I have never harmed you. Don't kill me,' she said.

'You have humiliated me, made me a figure of mockery,' shouted Gajanath and tried desperately to focus his glazed eyes on his victim.

Roopbala, adept at hiding herself from her husband's wrathful eyes, disappeared into the shadows at once. This angered him even more and he lurched forward blindly. Suddenly his foot caught the leg of the chair and he tripped over. The gun flew out of his hands and landed at Roopbala's feet. She stood staring at it in horror, and then, her instincts, inherited probably from the same Amazonian ancestor who had given her height, began to work. She leapt forward and grabbed the gun. 'You move back … or I … will shoot you,' she said, amazed at how loudly her voice came out. 'Go back,' she repeated and added, 'Please, I beg you …'

He was her husband, after all, and she was not going to kill him. Gajanath's eyes now bulged out of their sockets and he roared like a wounded, trapped tiger. He kicked at the chair to move it out of his way, but his strength was so ferocious and his aim so crooked that he drove the chair into the door and at the same time brought the curtain rod down. Roopbala didn't know what to do now. Her husband lay struggling under the heavy folds of a velvet curtain. She could hear his threats coming out in a choked, muffled voice as he tried to extricate himself. Then suddenly he lunged at her, still entangled in the velvet curtain, just his face and two eyes exposed. Roopbala held out the gun in front of her like a shield and Gajanath, thinking it was her arm, pulled it with all his might. The explosion shook the entire house and Roopbala hid her head in her hands. Paralysed with fear, she stood absolutely still. Then she opened her eyes and saw blood oozing out from under the curtain and she knew she had shot her husband dead. No sound came from the bundle and Roopbala did not dare to touch it.

All she could think of was running away from this blood-splattered velvet heap which was her late husband. Roopbala forced herself to think clearly. She knew she had to get away before it was daylight. Even now someone could have heard the shot and might come in to inspect. She ran into her room, quickly jumbled up a few clothes, snatched up the bag of jewellery she kept hidden under her bed, and after folding her hands to the garlanded pictures of gods, her late parents, and her in-laws, Roopbala fled into the dark night. She walked all the night, taking care to creep through standing crops of wheat till she had left the village boundaries behind. Now there was no danger of meeting any villager who would instantly recognize her as the landowner's wife. Just as the sky was getting lighter, she managed to catch a bullock-cart which would take her to the nearest town. Luckily Roopbala had some money tucked away in her sari end. It paid for her fare and one cup of tea. As soon as she reached the town, Roopbala sold her gold chain and bought herself a white sari. She found a secluded place near the river and there she broke the red glass bangles she always wore, cut her long hair off with a rusted razor blade, changed into white and officially declared herself a widow. She was only thirty-one years old. She went and sat down on the steps of a temple by the river and quietly began praying. Now began her endless search for peace of mind. Roopbala went from the small town to Allahabad to Benares to Mathura and finally to Hardwar. She sold all her jewellery, and when that money finished, she began living on alms.

Wherever she went, however much she prayed, Roopbala saw only her husband breathing his last. He came to her in her dreams regularly, shrouded in his velvet curtain, only his bloodshot eyes gleaming like two pieces of burning coal. 'Tall … witch … demon's daughter …' he shouted, his voice always muffled and low. Sometimes even when she was awake, Roopbala thought she saw him hovering near her elbow, but when she turned around sharply, there was no one there. Roopbala prayed all day long, asking god for forgiveness. She fasted on religious days and gave whatever little she had in charity, but her husband's spirit would not leave her. Roopbala grew thin and emaciated. She began to walk with an awkward stoop, which would have gladdened her late husband's heart had he seen it. A fanatical look had now come into her large eyes and her hands twitched nervously all the time. 'Penance, you have to do penance,' said the head guru of the ashram she had been staying at in Hardwar. 'Go to Badrinathji. There you

will find the peace you are searching for. Pray at the Lord's feet
and your husband's soul will be set free.'

Roopbala took his advice at once. She attached herself to a
party of old widows who were going up to Badrinath and they
agreed to let her come with them. 'She looks mad but she is
tall. She will help us on the mountain roads,' said the leader
of the group, a cheerful, plum-cheeked woman called Bela.

They set off one early morning, the three widows, Roopbala
and one short scowling man who seemed to be an old servant.
The women wore white like Roopbala, but they did not seem
to be like the ordinary widows Roopbala had met during her
wanderings in countless religious towns. These women had an
air of gaiety about them which was never seen in widows. They
chewed paan constantly, talked and laughed in loud voices, and
used strange words when they stumbled over a stone or their
servant did something wrong. The leader, Bela, was about fifty-
odd years and the other two, whose names Roopbala did not
know, because when she asked them they burst out laughing
for no reason and said, 'Call us what you want, sister,' were
younger. There were many other groups setting out for the
journey, but Roopbala chose to stay with these women because
they asked her no questions and accepted her quickly as one
of them. Maybe they too have committed some crime and are
going to seek forgiveness of Lord Vishnu, thought Roopbala
and a ghastly picture of three slain husbands instantly rose in
her mind. She began walking faster. The path was narrow and
full of stones but it was so well trodden that the surface was
smooth and the stones had no rough edges.

The pilgrims followed the river and Roopbala could often
hear loud cries of 'Jai Badrivishal … jai' rise above its deafening

roar. They walked slowly, but at a steady pace. The path allowed only one single file and behind them came the mules, loaded with all their belongings. Roopbala did not have anything to bring with her, except for a small bundle of two saris, but the other women had brought with them a huge amount of luggage. Besides their own personal belongings consisting of oils, soaps, clothes and paan boxes and many other items which far exceeded the limits an ordinary widow is allowed, thought Roopbala, the women also had huge bundles of cloth which they were going to give away to poor holy men on the way, and a pile of cooking pots which clanged at every step the mule took. Then there were dry rations of rice and dal, umbrellas, rush mats and pillows. A big, red cloth bag which contained the prayer books and rudraksha beads was kept separately from the worldly goods, and the servant, whose name was Ganesh, was often reprimanded if the two touched.

The path gradually began to get more and more steep and rocks jutted out at every corner like barriers. Roopbala had to brush aside the overhanging branches too, and she stumbled often. 'Be careful, sister, otherwise the river will take you back to where we came from,' laughed Bela and put an arm out to steady her. They walked till there was light and when the sun had disappeared behind the cliffs and they could no longer see the path, they settled down under a huge rock. The servant was instantly sent off to collect firewood and when he came back, grumbling loudly, showing the women the deep scratches on his arms, they just laughed and ordered him to start cooking. He huddled over the steaming pot, muttering angrily like an old witch brewing her evil potions. Roopbala sat separately, eating some parched rice she had brought with her, but the women forced her to share the food the servant had cooked. 'All your sins will be washed away soon, so why not eat with us?' said one of them mysteriously. Who are these women? wondered Roopbala once more as she ate the delicious, spicy vegetables after so many years of just boiled rice. Then mats were spread out on the ground and the women, tired out by the long journey, fell asleep at once. But Roopbala stared for a long time at the dark roof of the cave. She could hear jackals howling outside, and the river, glinting in the silvery moonlight, seemed to have quietened down now and flowed much more gently. Small black bats flew in and out of the cave and Roopbala watched their triangular shapes merge into the darkness. As usual, her dead husband's shrouded face appeared before her eyes and Roopbala gave a quiet sigh and went to sleep.

They started off early in the morning when the light was still not clear. A faint mist hung in the air and the path seemed to play hide and seek with them. It climbed higher and higher like a spiral of smoke and the women walked more slowly now. They would often stop, and then after taking a few deep breaths, start off again. The river had recovered its earlier fury and now raged below them, churning up waves and crashing them against the giant boulders. 'Do not look down,' shouted the coolie leading the mule. Roopbala looked straight ahead and walked, her knees trembling with fear. To add to her fright, the servant began telling them tales of horror he had heard from other pilgrims. 'One woman, a widow like you, fell down from right here. They found her in Hardwar. Had to cremate her there and then. Luckily, all the family were already present. Saved them the extra journey,' he said, looking pleased for the first time since they had left Hardwar. His good humour continued till they had reached the rock where they were to spend the night, and when the jackals began to howl, he at once started telling them stories about wild animals. 'There are bears here which attack only women for some reason. Sometimes panthers too come here at night, but if there is a man, they go away,' he said, as he served them their food. He was about to begin another tale when Bela sharply told him to keep quiet. The old man, hurt, walked out of the cave to his own sleeping place just outside, but before going, he cast a look of great horror, as if he could see something they could not. The women could not go to sleep even though they were weary and their legs ached. 'You go to sleep, I will keep watch,' said Roopbala, feeling sorry for them. Her words seemed to soothe them and they fell asleep after saying their prayers loudly.

Soon the cave echoed with their gentle snores and Roopbala sat up and watched the light playing on the cave walls. She thought of her past life and wondered how it would have been, had she been six inches shorter. Maybe she would have had children by now and would have been busy looking after them. Their family land had all been lost to payoff debts, but the small patch left would have been enough for her son. She could even see him running through the fields, his face a copy of her husband's, but a smiling, happy one, something she had never seen in him. Suddenly, a twinkling, bell-like sound came from the youngest woman's feet and Roopbala saw a quick gleam of a silver anklet before it disappeared under the bedclothes. She was stunned. No widow ever wore anklets or any other jewellery. Roopbala realized at once that these women were not respectable widows but bazaar women. Maybe they were dancing girls, or rather had been once, because they were too old now. She stared at their sleeping faces and slowly, in that dim moonlight, she began to see them differently. Their white saris changed into bright silken ones, and they lay there glittering with earrings, bangles, anklets, necklaces, nose pins and many other showy ornaments Roopbala imagined dancing girls wore to entertain their patrons. So that is what their sin is. But even then, mine is greater than theirs, she thought, unable to stop a feeling of slight pride creeping into her mind. She decided that she would walk much faster than them tomorrow and would not eat any more of their rich food. 'I am sure they eat garlic and onions.'

She shut her eyes and tried to go to sleep, forgetting her promise to guard over them. As always, her husband appeared, covered by the folds of the curtain, but this time he was accompanied by the three women who danced and swirled around the shapeless bundle. Roopbala watched the mirage play on her closed eyes and was about to fall asleep, when she heard a sudden grunt. She knew this was not a part of the dream because her husband had never made any sounds in the past five years that he had been regularly appearing, as soon as she shut her eyes. Roopbala opened her eyes and peered outside. The moon was covered by a fine strip of cloud and the river had turned into molten silver. And then a huge figure loomed at the entrance of the cave. It gave a low grunt and sat down. At first Roopbala thought it was a pilgrim who had lost his way and was looking for shelter. How tall he is, was her first thought. Maybe he too has no home like me. 'Have you lost your way, brother? There is a cave nearby where you can stay. We are only women here,' she said in a kind voice. The figure did not seem to understand what she was saying and was busy rummaging through the luggage, picking up boxes and sniffing them. It gave a low growl and Roopbala suddenly saw two hairy arms rise up in the air. It was a bear, she realized, and her heart stopped beating. The animal was now licking an empty pot and its claws made a horrible scratching sound on the metal. Roopbala watched it silently, not daring to breathe. The servant had said that the animal was scared of only men and she was afraid that it would see her and attack. Then she remembered that she was as tall as a man; her husband had always said so. 'A man she is, not my wife.' Roopbala gathered all her courage and stood up. She grabbed the umbrella and brought it down with all her might on the bear's head. She missed him by a long margin but hit the paan box hard. The clang was so deafening, it seemed to Roopbala, that her ears would burst. It echoed again and again, filling the small cave entirely, and a rubble of stones began to slide down from the roof. The women woke up screaming, but the bear had vanished long ago. Roopbala, feeling victorious and happy for the first time in her life, ran out to see where her enemy had fallen. But there was no trace of the animal. A sudden movement in the bushes caught her eyes and Roopbala went towards it, not afraid any more but eager to do battle. 'Oh god, save me … I will never cheat again … save me … I will give up tobacco … gambling … save me … oh god … have mercy …' moaned a voice and Roopbala moved the branches aside. Ganesh was huddled up there, shivering. He had covered his head with leaves and Roopbala reached out her hand to move them aside. 'Ohhh … nooo. I am a woman … only a woman …' he groaned, hiding his head deeper in the foliage. 'It is me … Roopbala. The bear has gone.' Ganesh sat quietly for a few moments and then leapt

out of the bush and fell at her feet. 'You are a goddess. You
have saved my life.' Roopbala was pleased by his gratitude but
did not want to show it.

She brushed him aside and walked back to the cave. 'What
was it?' asked the women, their eyes huge with terror. 'Oh
nothing, a bear. I chased it away.' As the women gasped in horror
mixed with admiration, Roopbala turned her smiling face to the
wall and went to sleep. Her husband's image, seeming to be too
affected by her bravery, faded away and did not show up again.

As soon as they woke up the next morning, Roopbala asked
the women who they were. At first they seemed reluctant to
say anything, but after Roopbala said she would be walking
separately from now on, they told her their story. 'We were the
Raja of Janigarh's dancing girls. All three of us were bought
by the Raja in Benares many years ago when we were mere
girls. Now we are old and cannot dance or sing any more, but
the Raja, a kind man, did not want to throw us out. He gave
us a cottage near the palace to live in and told us we could
sing devotional songs at his temple. Last year the Raja passed
away, so we discarded our fine clothes and jewels, shaved our
heads and came to pray for his soul,' said Bela.

'Do not leave us, sister, you have saved our lives. We were
never bad women, just singers and dancers like our mothers
were before us, and now we sing only to praise Lord Krishna,'
said the youngest one, whose anklet had given the secret away.
Roopbala, who was not keen to walk alone, said a few more
reluctant words just for appearance sake and then all of them
set off once more.

The path now curved dangerously as it wound its way up
the mountain. On one side, the Alaknanda river roared down

angrily, lashing at the boulders that stood in her way, and on the other side, the steep rocks rose like a wall. Sometimes the path was so narrow that Roopbala could only put one foot forward at a time. They walked very slowly now and none talked at all, because they were breathless with the effort of climbing. Ganesh trudged heavily behind her, huffing at every step. Whenever she turned around, his eyes looked pleadingly at her, imploring her to keep his secret. Roopbala liked the sense of power conquering the bear had given her, and gradually began to walk tall as she used to many years ago at home. The other pilgrims they passed on the way looked at her in awe as if she was some strange, mountain being, and even Bela treated her with more respect now.

The path continued as before, narrow, steep and strewn with stones, which made it more difficult to climb. Sometimes small stones rolled down from the cliffs above their heads and if they did not jump back quickly, they would land painfully on their heads. 'It is the road they are building for motor cars. That is what makes the mountain angry,' muttered Ganesh as they walked. 'If you want to go to the Lord's feet, you must walk there. What is the use of sitting comfortably in a motor car or a bus and reaching there? Badri Maharaj is benevolent to all, but I can tell you he will first answer the wishes of those who have walked all the way and then listen to those pilgrims who have come the easy way,' he announced to everyone they passed. The path became more difficult when it rained, but most of the time the sky was a clear blue and small clouds floated above their heads. It seemed to Roopbala that the same clouds from Hardwar were accompanying her to Badrinath.

As they climbed higher, the air became colder and Roopbala wrapped both her saris around her tightly. Bela and her sisters now began to distribute clothes to the many holy men who sat meditating on rocks along the way. They received the gift silently and only nodded their heads. But one man, meditating on a lonely rock, his long matted hair falling around him like a robe, shouted at them as soon as they came near. 'Go, you women of the devil, go, do not come here,' he screamed, raising his fist, his eyes shut tightly. The women scampered away but they left two dhotis by his side. Roopbala saw him pick up the clothes and examine them carefully just as they took the turn and left him.

'How did he recognize us with his eyes closed?' wondered the youngest sister, her voice full of admiration.

'Must be your stupid anklet, what else,' said her sister sharply.

'Why, it could be the smell of zarda in your paan,' she retorted at once.

'Old habits die hard,' muttered Ganesh from behind and then looked away sheepishly when Roopbala turned to look at him.

The sisters were more careful now and gave the dhotis only after examining the men. 'He should be very poor and thin. I do not like the look of these well-fed ones. A holy man can never be fat,' said Bela firmly and passed by several men who looked covetously at the bundle of new clothes. The women fed beggars too, and if they found astray pilgrim, suitably emaciated, they gave them money at once.

'God has given us so much, we must share it,' said Bela to Roopbala, but when her sister asked for a paan, she snatched her paan box away saying, 'Why did you not bring your own?'

The women quarrelled, sang devotional songs and gossiped with the other pilgrims they met. Sometimes they cried out loudly, beating their chests. 'What a man the Raja was! Give him peace. Oh Lord Badrivishal,' and then Roopbala too began to cry. She remembered her husband's angry face just before the curtain fell on him and her wails grew louder. The women, impressed, glanced at her.

The path now began to grow steep again and they all fell silent at once. For fifteen days they walked. Their faces were burnt black by the sun and their short hair now stood as matted as the holy men's. Roopbala's toenail had turned blue and now began to fall off. She had deep cuts on her feet where the sharp rocks had pierced and her face was lined with fatigue. But they still walked on, boasting how much each one was suffering. When Roopbala's nail finally fell off, a sign of envy appeared and each woman looked at her feet hopefully. 'The gods are watching to see how much we suffer, then they will reward us,' said Bela, smiling smugly when her hand was grazed by a thorn. Wild plants grew densely along the path, and when Roopbala looked up, she could she the high peaks towering above. Suddenly, for the first time in her entire life, Roopbala felt small. The tall deodar trees, the cascading waterfalls which fell from great rocky heights, the giant boulders that stood like small hills by the side of the river, and then above them all, the mighty snowcapped mountains, everything had been made for giants, much taller than her. 'This is where I should have been born. No one would feel offended by my height here,' she thought.

After walking for a few more hours, climbing wearily with tired, aching feet, they reached their destination at last. They could now hear the faint sound of bells ringing in the temple beyond and tried to walk as quickly as the narrow, uneven path allowed them. Though it had seemed so near, it was evening when they finally reached the gates of Badrinath. Roopbala could see the lamps glowing in the fading light and from the temple came the sound of a conch shell, as if it was calling her to prayer. She ran ahead, and then, as she bowed her head to touch the cool, stone step, she gave a soft sigh and fainted.

Roopbala lay unconscious and sick for many days after that but managed to survive somehow. The old dancing girls had nursed her through her nightmare and even now that she was well recovered, they sat looking at her with a maternal concern as if she was their newborn baby. 'Eat a little more. How pale you look,' they coaxed, taking turns to feed her, quarrelling over the best food for her. Even Ganesh hovered around, asking her gently if she wanted something, but disappeared at once when Bela ordered him to do some chore. Roopbala found that they were living in a hermitage not very far from the temple and she heard the soothing sounds of the chiming gongs. When she was feeling stronger, they went for a sight of the deity, and Roopbala sat on the steps and prayed for a long time. The crowds jostled her, and some people, thinking she was a beggar, even dropped a few coins in front of her, but she sat with her eyes closed, deep in meditation. The priests repeatedly asked her for money but she ignored them and they finally went away muttering, 'Widows are getting too clever these days.' She started coming to the temple every morning at dawn and sat on the steps, praying till the evening worship began. This was the time she liked best, when the smell of incense filled the air, the lamps were lit and conch shells began trumpeting. The low chanting of verses, though she could not understand a word, gave her a feeling of immense peace.

As days went by, Roopbala slowly forgot her past life, and the dark, frightening memory of her husband's dying scene gradually began to fade from her mind. Now when she shut her eyes, she only saw his scowling, stout figure just once in a while. 'Give, Ma, give one anna and you will find a place waiting for you in heaven. One anna, for you, two annas for your late husband and three annas for your parents and four annas for anybody else,' whispered a voice in honeyed tones, as if sharing a secret only with her. Roopbala opened her eyes and saw a young priest sitting nearby and watching her. She had never seen him before; he was too thin to be an experienced priest, but there was a wise look in his small, close-set eyes. She had been in Badrinath for a month now and had only prayed by herself. Now she was tempted to give this young priest one anna in case her own prayers were not enough when it came to getting a place in heaven. Then she thought why not include the entire family when she was going to pay. They could all achieve salvation together. Roopbala was about to speak to him, then she remembered that she had no money at all. Not even one anna for her own soul. She shook her head sadly and turned away. The priest seemed to understand and did not ask her again.

Roopbala now decided that she would try and earn enough money to buy her family their rightful places in heaven. 'I am here, so it is my duty,' she said. Bela and her sisters had left already, but even if they had been here she would not have asked them for money. Who knows what would happen if she used that kind of money for the prayers. Maybe god would send her entire family to hell to sing and dance for ever, thought Roopbala, a frown of worry appearing on her brow. 'No, I shall wash dishes at the hermitage or sweep the grounds; they will pay me one anna. That is all I want,' she said to herself. She began working from the very next day, and after a few months, earned her six annas for salvation. But the young priest whose face she found wise was not to be seen and Roopbala did not trust the older, fatter ones. So she continued to work, putting off the salvation ceremony for later.

One year passed, and Roopbala was still washing dishes and sweeping the hermitage courtyard. She had forgotten why she had started working. It seemed as if she was born to do this menial job. She had got used to it. She also began cleaning the temple steps on her own and polished them so hard that they shone like silver now. 'What a tall woman. She must be from a warrior caste,' thought the priest and allowed her to clean the outer rooms too. It was difficult to find someone to do the work, and moreover, she was not asking for more than one anna. Gradually she started selling flowers and leaves for the worship to the pilgrims, charging the wealthy ones but giving them away free to poor people.

One day when Roopbala was collecting the old flower petals to put them under the tree, she saw a stocky man climbing up the temple steps. She stopped working and stood still her heart was beating very fast. How could this be? Had she gone mad or was god punishing her again for her sins? The man came closer and then sat down with a loud grunt. His face was turned away from her but she knew without doubt that it was her late husband. Who else could express so much resentment in a single, low grunt? Roopbala's legs began to tremble, but she forced herself to go forward. 'Do you want some flowers?' she asked, her voice coming in a harsh whisper. He looked up at her but his eyes seemed to be glazed over with a film of cataract. He did not recognize her. Then she noticed he had only one arm. A series of horrifying thoughts raced through her mind as Roopbala stood staring at him. Suddenly a woman came up to them. 'So you are here. How many times have I told you to stay behind me, not walk so fast? Are you deaf as well as blind?' she said in a shrill, scolding voice. Roopbala was amazed to see Gajanath just bow his head and say nothing. 'What has happened to his mighty rage?' she thought. Then they both got up and walked away, Gajanath taking care to stay two steps behind the woman. Roopbala heard her say, 'You were giving the tall beggar woman money, weren't you? You fool. Wasting our money.'

Roopbala wanted to call out to him but she stopped. What was the use now, she thought, and stood silently watching them. The woman was so short that Gajanath, even with his hunched up, cringing posture, looked like a giant next to her. 'God grants all our wishes eventually, but still you can't have everything,' thought Roopbala and laughed. Suddenly she knew she had been set free and let the peace of Badrinath engulf her once more.

Life in a Palace

WHEN GITA'S HUSBAND DISAPPEARED ONE NIGHT QUIETLY, LEAVING only a smudged one-line note saying he was renouncing the world to become a holy man, she too suddenly decided to break away. 'I shall go to Nagpur and find a job,' she said, taking an independent decision for the first time in her life. Her family, consisting of one fierce and dominating mother-in-law, a set of equally aggressive parents, two highly placed and pompous brothers-in-law on either side and two demanding sisters, all rose up and protested in one voice. 'What will people say?' was their first reaction, followed by a chest-thumping: 'Are we paupers that you have to work?' This was the first time they had jointly disagreed on the same point and the two indignant households merged into one raging inferno. Gita was shouted at, lectured to, and even threatened with starvation if she mentioned leaving home again. Gita let their anger simmer down, and when their united opposition began to crack and they were once again preoccupied by their old vendettas, she quietly stole out of the house one evening, just as her husband had done.

Carrying only one small cloth bag and two soiled, hundred-rupee notes which she had found amongst her husband's discarded worldly goods, Gita walked to the station and bought a ticket to Nagpur. She could only whisper the name of her destination when she asked for the ticket and her knees were trembling so much that she had to hold on to the wooden ledge as she paid the money. She kept looking over her shoulder all the time, expecting to find all her four brothers-in-law running towards her from different directions. Every voice that spoke near her seemed to belong to some member of her family, and once she was quite sure she saw her father approaching the ticket counter, but when the man was pushed aside by another hurrying passenger, she sighed with relief, because she knew that her father would always make sure he had the right of way. Once when they were travelling to Calcutta, her father had stood with one arm across the door and not allowed a single passenger get on to the train till not only he and his family, but the entire coach had disembarked. Gita still remembered the abuses of those passengers as they stamped their feet angrily on the platform, but such was the power of her father's mesmerizing gaze that not one person tried to push the frail old man aside and jump on to the train. Gita did not want to meet those eyes now, because if she did, she knew she would just turn around and go back home, never to step out again.

Holding her bag tightly, taking a deep breath, she plunged into the crowd as if it were an ocean waiting to swallow her up. Everyone seemed to know where they were going, except for her. She shuffled along vaguely, working up enough courage to ask someone, when she suddenly heard a man nearby tell his wife, 'Bombay Mail to Nagpur is leaving from platform six.' She knew that was her train, and from then on, Gita hung on to that particular couple, following them closely as they wove their way through the teeming, pushing crowd. For one panic-stricken moment she thought she had lost her guides, but then she saw the man's head emerge out of the wave of people and she rushed towards him, smiling with relief. The man caught her glance and looked away quickly. But his wife stopped in her tracks and Gita almost bumped headlong into her. 'Who is she?' the woman asked, turning her face in one swift movement to assess Gita and at the same time cast a glowering look at her husband. The man began walking faster, wearing an expression of such intense guilt that Gita thought for a moment that she really knew him. Then the crowd swallowed them, but before they were lost for ever, Gita heard the woman's voice rise shrill and clear above the din of the station. 'Father of four brats … you will not change your habits. At your age …'

Gita decided now that it was safer to follow a coolie. She ran behind an old coolie trudging ahead with a mountain of luggage, and after she had caught up with him, asked him the way to platform six. When he said, 'Follow me, didi,' Gita almost held his arm, she was so scared to lose this kind mentor. Gita had never travelled alone anywhere, and in fact, she had never done anything alone or independently. Ever since she could remember, someone had told her what to do and she had always obeyed them happily. She had never bathed in hot water, because her grandfather, a great believer in nature cure, has asked her not to. She had learnt fifty English poems by heart because her father, a committed Anglophile, had ordered her to and then she had not recited them in public because her grandmother, a deeply religious lady, had told her not to speak in a mlechcha or barbarian tongue. She learnt how to sing, do water-colour paintings and play the sitar because her mother said it would get her a good husband, but when she got married and her mother-in-law declared, 'No daughter-in-law of mine is going to sing and dance like a bazaar woman,' Gita promptly stopped. She cooked all the meals, though there were three servants in the house, because her father-in-law said, 'A daughter-in-law looks good in the kitchen.' Only her gentle, dreamy-eyed husband had never asked her for anything, except to be left alone to meditate. But he had gone now for ever and she knew she too had to break away before it was too late. So, with her trembling, uncertain hands, she had seized the opportunity. She knew it would be difficult to start life again at forty-two, but she hoped her old school friend in Nagpur would help her out somehow.

But now as she stood staring helplessly at the frantic, rushing crowd and the mad chaos of the station, her courage began to fail her and she wanted to go back home. Just then someone pushed her roughly and Gita stumbled. She looked down and saw that her bag was missing. She tried to call out but no sound came from her throat. She stood there mutely as tears rolled down her cheeks. This would have never happened to any member of her family. No thief would ever dare to rob them, thought Gita. Suddenly, a fat, white arm caught her and shook her.

'Can't you be careful? Here is your bag. Move on, girl. Don't sleep in the middle of the station. You just attract thieves,' her saviour said.

Gita looked through a haze of tears and saw one of the fattest but most beautiful women she had ever seen. Large, almond-shaped green eyes stared at her with irritation but smiled indulgently at the same time. The lady was dressed in an expensive silk sari but her blouse was torn all along the sleeve.

Huge diamonds glittered in her ears and one single stone shone like a beacon on her well-shaped nose. Her hair was gathered up in an untidy bun and the pins were about to drop.

'Are you dumb or what? Here, take my bag; you don't have anything to carry. Hold it properly,' she said and thrust an untidy bundle of clothes at her. Gita, trained to obey orders like an old soldier, took the bundle at once and began to follow the lady into the train. Her moment of weakness had passed and she did not feel so scared any more. 'This lady will show me where my seat is,' thought Gita, feeling much better, now that she had someone to obey. Behind them, two old women, dressed in white, hovered anxiously. But the old lady pushed them away, saying, 'You go to the third class. Don't follow me. Remember to get out at Raipur. I won't bring you back this time from Nagpur,' she said and heaved herself up the steps. As soon as she entered the train, she began calling out in a booming voice, 'Binu, Shanu, where are you?' Her voice filled the entire train and her massive figure did not allow anyone to pass as she ambled down the corridor. She kept walking into every compartment, and then, after giving the occupants a thorough inspection, backed out again, still shouting, 'Binu … Shanu …' At last they found the right compartment and Gita saw two pretty, bejewelled women who were obviously Binu and Shanu, sitting in one corner and playing cards.

They did not reply or even look up when the lady came in, though they must have heard her thundering voice a long time ago. 'Look, who has come,' said the lady and produced Gita like a prized hunting trophy. One of the women gave Gita an indifferent look and went back to her card game.

'You cheat,' she screamed suddenly, and from the power of her voice and her perfect profile, Gita knew she must be the old lady's daughter. 'I look up for one minute and you pick up a card. And ace at that,' she cried and then reached forward and grabbed the other woman's hair. Her victim retaliated at once and slapped her hand soundly. Gita stared at them in horror. She had never seen grown-up women fight like this. But the old lady ignored them and sat down heavily on the seat, 'Put the clothes down on the box. You sit here with me. I am the Rani-ma of Jussalpur. What is your name? Are you running away from home? A bit old for that, aren't you?' said the lady, rapidly firing questions at her and at the same time taking out four small paans, one after another, from an old silver box and stuffing them greedily into her mouth.

'He ran away from me ... to the Himalayas,' said Gita, speaking for the first time, her voice unnaturally loud.

'Some people have all the good luck,' said one of the daughters, giving Gita a friendly look now. 'My fool of a husband will not even go to the market, he is so scared of getting lost,' she said. 'Now that you are here, why don't you play cards with us?' Her sister nodded eagerly. Gita went and sat near them and noticed for the first time that they were identical twins, but since one was very fat, like her mother, while the other one was painfully thin, they did not look alike from afar. But sitting together face to face, they looked like the same person and Gita was suddenly reminded of a picture she had seen in an English magazine for weight-reducing pills. 'Before and after', it had said.

'I do not know how to play cards,' she mumbled, feeling shy all of a sudden.

'We shall teach you. Anyway, we have our own rules,' they said together and looked gleefully at each other like two cats who had put aside their old enmity and decided to share a mouse.

'No, no, she cannot play cards … she has to take me to the toilet,' said Rani-ma and grabbed Gita's arm. 'Quick … let us go,' she gasped, rolling her eyes and puffing out her already bloated cheeks even more. Gita, fearing there was some kind of an emergency on hand, quickly escorted her out of the compartment. But all that the old lady wanted to do was spit the paan juice out of the window. Then, pushing Gita aside, she waddled to the toilet. 'You stay here. I might get stuck, then open the door and pull me out,' she said and went into the toilet.

Gita knew this was a good chance to escape from this mad lady and her strange daughters and go and look for her own seat on the train. But she was so fascinated by the old Rani, so taken in by her strange ways, that she could not bring herself to leave her. It was like tearing oneself away from an exciting play before it had ended. Gita wanted to know more about her and find out who exactly she was and where she was going. She had never before felt this kind of curiosity about anyone in her life and was surprised at herself.

Suddenly there was a loud hammering on the door. Gita twisted the handle and pushed. The old lady's massive figure was stuck between the basin and the half-open door, just as she had predicted. But obviously it had happened many times before, because she gave Gita precise instructions, step by step, on how to pull her out. 'Hold my arms first. Turn my body. Now push the door slowly with your foot. Good … now move back and pull harder. Hold tight …' she said, barking out orders like a sergeant-major at drill. Gita obeyed the instructions at once, feeling very much at home. Slowly, inch by inch, the lady emerged from the bathroom as Gita pushed and pulled, and after one final wriggle, she came out with a loud pop. 'Oh ... What a trial ... Why do they make the toilets so small? These British wanted to save money on everything ... They always thought we were a nation of dwarfs,' she said angrily, rubbing her back. 'In my father's state, the train had bathrooms as big as the compartment. Our servant travelled just next door to us, not like this. But now we are no longer rulers and have to suffer like you ordinary people. God knows where my maids are sitting,' she said. They walked back to the compartment and once more the old lady stopped and peered rudely into every open door before moving on. 'If your husband has run away to become a holy man, why don't you come and work for me? I need a companion and I like your face. It is as stupid as a cow's, but honest,' she said as soon as she sat down. Gita muttered that she wanted to go to Nagpur and work. 'Who will give you work at your age? You don't even look healthy or strong or clever. Your in-laws will never take you back and your parents will not be happy to have you for ever. Look at me, stuck with two married daughters at home, along with their good-for-nothing husbands,' she said. Her daughters tittered loudly and carried on playing cards.

'You come with us to Jussalpur; we shall teach you eighty-two different card games,' said the thin one.

'Our father is the Raja. He keeps bees, our brother is a drunkard, but a very good hunter when he is sober. His wife is a stupid woman with ugly teeth that stick out, but she stays in her parents' house most of the time. Our husbands are equally useless and stupid, but you will hardly ever see them. They are very scared of people and stay hidden on the top floor of our palace,' said the fat one, describing the joys of Jussalpur eagerly.

'Come with us, you will really like it there. We have five ponds full of fish and our mango orchards have the best fruit,' said Rani-ma, and assuming the matter had been settled, stretched herself out on the berth and went off to sleep promptly.

The daughters continued playing cards, occasionally hissing at each other in low voices. Gita sat quietly and thought. For the first time in her life she had had the courage to set herself free from her overpowering family. Did she want to go and live with these strange women? Why not? It would be safer than being in Nagpur, where so many of her relatives lived. They would find her and report her to her family at once. Yes, she would go with them, stay for a few months till things were safer. Gita, pleased, now that she had made a second independent decision so well and so quickly, sat back contentedly. The train was passing through a dense forest and all that Gita could see was a wall of golden brown leaves. Even the floor of the forest was covered by the leaves and not a single green plant could be seen anywhere. Gita peered into the forest and saw a dim, yellow light blinking far away. Was it an animal or a man, she wondered, feeling a bit frightened. What if she got lost in a forest like this, she thought morbidly and looked away with a shiver.

Rani-ma was sleeping peacefully, her head rolling awkwardly on one side as if it had been chopped off, while the daughters had packed up the cards and were now fiddling with the largest tiered tiffin box Gita had ever seen. Binu or Shanu, she still had not worked out who was who, opened a container and quickly began pulling out a stack of pooris. 'Come, eat,' she whispered and poured a stream of curry into a bowl. She opened the boxes one by one and laid them out near her. Her sister quickly reached out and slid them towards her. They glared at each other and then began eating, dipping their pooris into the containers at top speed, as if they were racing with each other. Gita wanted to wake up Rani-ma, who was now snoring gently, her head still in the lolling, guillotined position, but her daughter said, 'Let her be. She will finish all the food.' Gita was shocked. She could not believe her ears. How could they treat their mother like that? She shook the old lady's arm gently and said, 'Rani-ma ... please have ...' but before she could finish the sentence, the old lady leapt up and snatched the pooris out of her hand. Holding them in her fat palm, she swept up the entire contents of one container of curry in one clean swoop. Then, as Gita watched with her mouth open, she polished off the pooris, four at a time, along with all the curry. Her daughters made quick swipes at the food but only managed to get one or two half-torn pooris or a bit of the curry.

Gita had lost her appetite entirely and just sat back and watched them. It was dark when they finally finished eating and not a morsel of food was left in the two-foot-high tiffin box. 'The trouble with not having the maids here is that you can only carry a small amount of food,' complained the old lady with a sigh as she watched the tiffin box being closed. They went to sleep at once, not bothering to clean the tiffin box or pack the utensils. Gita quietly did everything and then lay down on her berth. She was sure she would not be able to sleep, since this had been the most eventful day in her life, but soon she was fast asleep herself. When they woke up, the train was about to reach Raipur.

'What a pity, there is nothing left to eat,' said Rani-ma looking sad.

'Check in the other compartment, perhaps someone will give us something,' said the fat daughter.

When Gita, horrified, refused to go, she sauntered off herself and came back clutching four oranges and a few bananas. They ate them slowly, as if to make the fruit last till the train reached the station. It was still dark, but Gita could see faint streaks of a silvery light in the sky. As soon as the train stopped, a crowd of women rushed into their compartment and began touching Rani-ma's feet. 'Are you all right? How did you eat? You poor things, how you must have suffered,' they said in whining tones, clicking their tongues. Rani-ma gave them the luggage to carry, saying, 'Did you bring tea?' and slowly moved out of the compartment as if the train was going to stop here for ever. Gita nervously followed her, trying not to push her from behind. There were more servants waiting outside on the platform, along with two stern-looking guards. They formed a corridor, and Rani-ma, followed by her daughters and Gita, marched out of the station. The ticket collector at the gate made no effort to check their tickets, and only bowed low with folded hands. The light had become clearer now and the old station building glimmered as if it were made of silver paper. Two battered, ancient cars stood right outside, and after some initial confusion about where the basket of sweets, which had suddenly appeared from nowhere, was to go, they were on their way to Jussalpur.

Gita sat between the sisters, who began quarrelling at once about the score of their last card game. The driver, a scrawny, old man, joined in their bickering too, as if he had been present all through the game, and kept turning around as he drove recklessly over the bumpy road. Gita's head was now aching and she wondered if she had done the right thing. Then she remembered her family and knew she had taken the right step. They travelled slowly, stopping often to eat from various tiffin boxes and baskets, which the servants kept producing. The sun beat angrily down on their heads and the old car rattled so loudly and persistently that Gita thought it would break down any minute. But they bumped along steadily, passing fields of green wheat and groundnut. There were vast empty acres of red earth where giant rocks stood like walls and then again suddenly a thick forest would appear. After many bone-breaking, dusty miles, they finally reached Jussalpur. Gita saw a small town, full of cropped white-and-green houses, sprawling untidily among giant rocks, and at one far end, hidden behind a curtain of tall trees, stood the palace. It seemed to Gita that it leaned drunkenly on one side and she wondered if her eyesight was beginning to play tricks on her. But then Rani-ma said, 'There it is, still standing. You know, there is a pond underneath, and every year our palace sinks a few inches into it. Good you came now, otherwise it would have been too late,' she added laughing.

The cars seemed to have acquired a new burst of energy as they entered their own territory and roared through the narrow lanes of the town, blaring their horns. Gita saw men bow low and then turn their faces away. 'They are not supposed to see us,' said Binu. 'But we can see them,' she added, grinning coquettishly. As soon as they reached the palace, a fresh batch of servants rushed to take over, shouting excited greetings, touching Rani-ma's feet, and out of the confusion, a parrot suddenly flew across and settled on Rani-rna's shoulders. 'Ah, my Mithu, my son. How are you?' cooed the old lady as the bird tweaked her ear. 'Wretched old fool, still alive. How many times I have wrung its neck,' said Shanu, glaring at the bird.

Rani-ma now began walking down the corridor which led into the house, issuing orders to the servants, scolding them in an affectionate voice. Gita was not sure of what she should do, since Rani-ma seemed to have forgotten about her, so she stood uncertainly for a few moments and then, panic-stricken, quickly started following her. But by then, Rani-ma seemed to have disappeared into the walls, along with her retinue. Gita could hear her voice still shouting, but she could not see anyone at all. She walked down the long corridor, searching for her. Room after room with no one in it opened out before her. None of them had any furniture, but the walls and ceilings were covered with faded paintings. Gita moved like a sleep-walker through the empty rooms, tracing her fingers on the dusty, cobweb-covered walls. Then suddenly the rooms ended and she founded herself standing in front of a huge, open courtyard.

It was shaded by old trees and a fountain stood forlornly in the middle and a row of boxes stood neatly along the edge. A very old man with a long, white beard was bending over one of the boxes and talking loudly to someone. 'My beautiful queen, how fat you are getting every day. The workers are looking after you well. Good. Good. Eat well,' he shouted. Gita, quite sure that he was talking to Rani-ma, went ahead quickly to find her. But there was no one there. The old man heard her footsteps and turned around. 'Who are you? A spy?

Has Rani-ma sent you to steal my queen?' he said, shouting. Gita realized this must be the beekeeper—the Raja. She bent down and touched his feet. The old man, frightened, took a step back. 'I thought you were going to hit me,' he said, smiling sheepishly now. 'No one touches my feet any more. I am the Raja, I tell them. The British used to pay me a huge pension. The new raj gives me only a pittance. Do you know, my father even got a gun-salute once. People say it went off by mistake, but it was still a salute,' said the old man, looking so dejected that Gita thought he was going to burst into tears. But then he brightened up suddenly. 'Want to see my queen? Not scared of bees, are you, young girl?' Gita was petrified of all flying insects ever since a wasp had gone into her hair. It had buzzed away happily for hours and no one dared to take it out. Eventually she had had to put her head above burning logs to smoke it out. But she did not want to hurt this gentle-eyed old man and, clenching her fists, followed him to the box. The bees hummed angrily as they worked and the Rajasahib began cooing to them. 'What if they flew out and got stuck in his beard?' thought Gita. She stood stiffly for a few frightening moments and then moved away quietly. The Raja did not even notice that she had gone and now began singing to the bees in a surprisingly beautiful voice. Gita sat down in the shade of the tree and listened. A feeling of peace came over her as she watched the old man and she shut her eyes and fell asleep.

'Is she dead? Why did Ma pick such an unhealthy one this time?' a voice said, and Gita opened her eyes and sat up. She was still sitting under the tree but Rajasahib had disappeared and a strange man with red-rimmed eyes was staring at her angrily. A strong smell of alcohol came out of him as he said, 'She is alive; thank god. I could not stand a funeral in this heat,' and began walking away, still glaring at her. Gita wanted to ask him where Rani-ma was, but before she could, the man tripped over the ledge and fell flat on his face. Gita gave a loud gasp, but the man did not cry out or try to get up. He just folded his hands under his head and made himself comfortable. Looking up at the sky he said, 'Are you a widow, an unmarried mother, a bad woman, or an escaped convict? Or are you some new kind ... my mother likes new faces. I like old ones. You do not have to remember their names ... Why have names at all?' he said, lifting his head a little to look at Gita. 'Take my name. Shishirdeo Bhandeo Gajapatnath Devkumar Singh. But what do they call me? Bolu. Waste. A total waste. Four men could have used my name. What is your name?' he asked, suddenly sitting up. Gita did not wish to talk to him. He was a drunkard; she remembered his sister had said so on the train, so she kept quiet. 'Ah. A deaf and dumb one this time. Poor soul, but at least she won't jabber away like the last one. How much that woman talked, especially in the mornings when my head is so sensitive to sounds. Good thing the tiger got her,' he muttered, smiling to himself. Then he got up unsteadily and wandered away, still laughing.

Gita decided to trace her way back to the entrance, in case Rani-ma or her daughters were there. After a few false turns, she found a maid who led her to Rani-ma. 'I thought you had run away,' she said as soon as she saw Gita and hugged her joyously. Then, giving her a large bowl of rabri to eat, she turned around to some ladies who were sitting with her and announced proudly, 'This is the new one. Her husband has abandoned her to become a holy man. I saved her from a gang of robbers and brought her here. Her name … What's your name?' asked Rani-ma in a low voice. Gita told her name and was cheered lustily by the ladies present as if she had said something profound. She was accepted at once by the huge, floating, female population of the palace and everyone seemed to know her entire history and she received looks of sympathy wherever she went.

In a few days, Gita learnt the layout of the palace and could find her way about easily. Rani-ma treated her with a kind of absent-minded affection and though Gita was supposed to be her companion, she saw her only for a few hours in the morning. 'Read some religious book to me,' the old lady would say, chewing her paan or eating from her endless store of sweets, 'but make sure it is short. Some of them go on for ever. Even god would not have time to listen to such endless sagas.' Gita would read her a short passage from the Ramayana or Mahabharata, and she would sit impatiently, drumming her fingers, or teasing the parrot that sat watching them from her shoulders. Sometimes she would argue with Gita about what she read, but then she would quickly fold her hands over the book and ask for forgiveness in a worried voice. Once her brief duty to religion was over and done with, both would sit down to eat a huge, many-course meal and then Rani-ma would disappear to do mysterious chores around the house. The daughters stayed in their rooms and played cards. Gita would often hear screams and abuses emerging from the room and once she even saw a velvet slipper fly. She had not met the shy, reclusive sons-in-law as yet, but the brother roamed the house at night, crashing into furniture and cursing loudly. The buck-toothed sister-in-law had apparently gone visiting. Gita went and sat with the old Raja every afternoon and sometimes even sang to the bees with him.

Weeks passed by peacefully and soon Gita forgot what her earlier life was like. Her bullying, demanding, domineering family gradually faded into the past and Gita had no desire to leave Jussalpur and look for a job in Nagpur. She had not been paid any salary as yet, but then she had no need for money. Rani-ma had given her a big bundle of saris but warned her not to tell her daughters. 'They will snatch them away. Hide them.' The daughters had given up playing cards and had taken up ballroom dancing now. They had a gramophone and a few scratched records in an old trunk and now music blared day and night from their room. The old instrument had to be wound up every few minutes and Gita was put in charge. She also had to change the needle after each record and be the referee, since the daughters constantly fought over which record should be played. In fact, Binu had already stabbed Shanu once in her back with a needle when she refused to take her record off. They were learning to dance from a book which had been translated from English by someone who had no clue whatsoever what the purpose of these strange exercises was. As a result, the instructor seemed to be as confused as his pupils and the two women, already mismatched by their extremely fat and thin bodies, constantly tripped over each other or got entangled in a complicated wrestling hold. To add to their troubles, the gramophone would suddenly slow down in mid-song and begin to wail in an eerie, hair-raising voice. Once it set up a howl just as the brother was passing outside the room. 'Let me go, save me ...' he cried suddenly and then they heard a loud thud. They rushed out and found him stretched out on the floor, waving his hands, his eyes wide open with fear. 'Go, go,' he kept saying in a feeble voice, as if someone or something were standing over him.

The ballroom dancing fad lasted for a long time and even Rani-ma got interested in it. She got hold of an Anglo-Indian lady who lived in Jussalpur town, to come and teach the daughters properly. The lady turned up one morning, dressed in a frilled white frock and spotless white gloves. The entire household, except for Rajasahib, came to look at her, and for the first time, Gita saw the two sons-in-law emerge in the daylight. The dance teacher, Mrs Pewtin, was escorted into the dance room by Rani-ma herself and everyone settled down to watch. Gita put a record on and the old gramophone groaned into life. 'My Bonnie lies over the ocean ... My Bonnie lies over the sea ...' it sang loudly, just slightly off-key. 'Oh bring back ... Oh bring back ... Bring back my Bonnie to meee ...' as Mrs Pewtin swirled around the room, holding Binu in her arms. 'Step one, step one ... two,' she called out in a soft musical voice. Rani-ma gazed upon them fondly and even Shanu was smiling for once. Everything was going well and Binu was beginning to get the hang of the dance, when the bees decided to join the fun. No one knew what exactly happened, how they got out of their box and came so far into the palace. All they knew was that they were there. The first person they attacked was poor Mrs Pewtin, as if they knew she was an outsider, then they flew in one straight line towards Binu, and stung her on her arms. Shanu's huge figure loomed ahead and the bees left her skinny sister and clung to her. Gita was stung on her hands and the women who had come to watch did not escape either.

Only Rani-ma sat still and the bees avoided her carefully. Everyone else ran around crying, shouting, waving their sari ends and jamming the narrow doorway. Even the gramophone was affected by the trauma around it and the needle got stuck, '... Bring back ... Bring back ... Bring back ...' it kept repeating in a hollow, despairing voice. Then suddenly it could stand it no longer and began to wail. It had never howled so emotionally as it did now. Mrs Pewtin, who had been running around in circles trying to get out, now froze. The bees too stopped their frenzied battle and began buzzing in a surprised tone. Then, as the gramophone screeched and wailed, they quickly flew out of the door and disappeared as quietly as they had come. Mrs Pewtin ended the drama by gracefully fainting on the carpet. Rani-ma's parrot, who had been dozing throughout, now screeched angrily and flew down to settle on her white gloved hand.

The dancing mania came to an abrupt end after this and Rani-ma banned any kind of English music in the palace because she felt this was what had angered the bees. 'The Raja sings only classical notes to them. They do not like English or foreign songs,' she said. The Raja, of course, did not know what had happened and continued to coo notes of bhairavi to his beloved bees. Gita was now told to teach the daughters devotional songs and a tanpura was installed in the very same place where the unfortunate gramophone had perched in its heyday. Every morning they sat down to sing and Gita was surprised to see how quickly they picked up the songs. She gradually began talking to them about literature and found a book of Kalidasa's poems for them to read. The daughters instantly took to poetry as a parched plant sucks in water, and from then on, began reading whatever they could find in their father's library. There were hundreds of dusty, moth-eaten books there and Gita saw that many of them were quite valuable. She cleaned them carefully and put them back in order. She also began doing accounts for Rani-ma and giving money to the servants. Gita, who had been so timid and uncertain at home, found herself in charge of this rambling household and it amazed her to see how even Rani-ma listened to her advice.

A year had gone by and Gita often thought of her family. She wanted to write to her mother, but kept putting if off. One night she made up her mind, and after everyone had gone to sleep, she sat down in the library with a blank sheet of paper. She could not think of a single thing to say. She thought hard and then she suddenly heard a whimper. Thinking it was a rat, Gita ignored it, but the sound gradually became louder. It was a human voice. Now another voice spoke up, stumbling over the words, 'You are my ... friend ... come have ... have drink.' Gita recognized it as Bolubana, the drunken son's voice. She quickly got up to leave the room before he could find her. But then she peered out and saw that he was sitting on the veranda outside the library. He was holding a thin, dark man by his throat and urging him to drink. 'Drink, my friend ... you know I have no friends ... you ... you stay here with me ... you want a cigar to smoke ... you stay here ... my friend ...' he said, slurring his words. 'Please ... huzoor, let me go, please ... sahib,' whimpered the man, trying to shake off Bolubana's hands. But the drunken man's grip was as tight as a newborn baby's, and the man clawed helplessly at his throat. 'I will never steal again ... please, mai-baap ... send me to jail, call Rani-ma ... ma ...' he gasped, his eyes now bulging out with terror. 'Who dares to send my friend to jail?' shouted Bolu, shaking the man violently. 'I will kill them. I am, I am a prince of Jussalpur … Jussalpur's prince.' In his fervour to prove his royalty by thumping his chest, Bolu had let go of one hand. The thief seized the opportunity and slipped out of his clutches. He began running wildly towards the steps. 'Where … where are you … my friend … so lonely,' Bolubana cried out dejectedly, groping in the dark for his friend's throat. But the man had already fled into the palace gardens. Gita could hear him shouting: 'Santri … babu … help.'

It was after this incident that Bolubana started seeing visions. Earlier, after a heavy bout of drinking, he used to see all kinds of strange animals and beings, but now he began to see things on a grand scale, even when sober. In fact, the new visions shook him up so much that he totally stopped drinking, but they continued to haunt him. Armies on horses charged straight at him, elephants picked him up and threw him down suddenly, without warning, men with swords lashed out at him from hidden corners and the earth caved in under him as soon as he got out of bed. But as time went on, instead of being frightened by these happenings, Bolubana began to enjoy them. He described each vision in detail and with great drama. His two sisters, his mother, Gita and the servants began to follow him around, not wishing to miss out on any new vision. In fact, the word got around, and people from the surrounding villages came to see him. Long queues formed at the palace gates and Rani-ma seized the opportunity and began charging everyone two paise. Bolubana had never got such attention in his life and was enjoying himself thoroughly. Even his estranged wife returned, curious to see the visions her husband was recounting. Gita suddenly realized that he was lying. He had probably seen one drink-induced vision a long time ago and was cashing in on that till now, as well as adding new ones from his imagination. But people were now pouring into the palace from far away villages to see Bolubana. Jussalpur had never been so crowded before and the sweetmeat-sellers did brisk business. 'Bless our Bana sahib,' they said each morning. Bolu, in a flowing silk robe, would appear twice a day in the topmost balcony of the palace, like a medieval king, and wave to the people. Then he would raise his face to the sky and rattle off a series of visions he could see. Then as the crowd sighed and shook their heads in wonder, he would turn around and go back into his room, take off the robe and sit down to play cards.

The visions ended in the same place, at the same time as they had begun, exactly one year later. Bolubana got up one night, feeling thirsty. Shouting out exact details of whatever he saw was tiring him out and his throat was constantly parched. He wished he had not given up drinking. He found the jug in his room empty, so he walked out into the veranda to drink water from the large earthen pot kept there. Two golden eyes gleamed at him out of the darkness and suddenly a large black panther sprang down from the tree in front of him. 'Bagh, help … bagh … on the tree …' he screamed in a voice very different from the one he used to talk to his audience. But the servants, now quite fed up with the daily sightings of strange beings, just turned around and went back to sleep. Luckily for Bolubana, the panther was not keen to eat human flesh and slunk back into the forest after it had given the shivering, shaking Bolubana a good look. This was one vision Bolubana did not talk about, and in fact, refused to see anything any more. Gita was relieved when the palace grounds were empty once more and she started teaching the palace women how to read and write. Binu and Shanu helped her and even persuaded their husbands to correct the exercise books when the classes were over.

Two years had now passed and Gita thought of going home once to see her mother. Rani-ma, her two daughters, Bolubana, and even Rajasahib got ready to go with her. In fact, they got their trunks ready and Rani-ma at once began ordering food that they would need for the journey. The idea of the two sides clashing, with her in the middle, was so frightening and unnerving for Gita that she changed her mind and only wrote to them telling them she was well and happy and had no wish to return ever. Life at the palace was moving at its usual, sleepy pace, punctuated with odd happenings as usual. At the moment the excitement was over, a new wig that Rani-ma had ordered from England. The old lady had looked in the mirror one morning and decided that she was going bald. 'It is because of Rajasahib's curses,' she insisted and immediately sent for a fancy hairpiece. The orders must have got mixed up somewhere, because when the box arrived at the palace and was opened, a bright, gleaming, red wig was found nestling in tissue paper. Everyone gave a gasp of dismay, but Rani-ma bravely announced that she would wear it. 'I have paid good money for it. Why should I not wear it?' she declared, quelling any criticisms of the wig. But when she strode out the next morning, the flaming wig sitting lopsidedly on her regal head, they gaped in horror. Even the parrot gave a hysterical shriek and would not sit on her shoulder any more. The servants stared from afar at their old mistress with fear, as if she had turned into a witch and avoided her. Gita too did not have the courage to tell her how terrible she looked and did not meet her eyes when she spoke to her. The daughters just laughed rudely, calling her 'the red devil', but Bolubana, after he had bumped into her in one dimly-lit corridor, gave a loud scream, and certain that the visions had returned, at once began drinking again. Rajasahib could not be convinced that she was his wife and attacked her with a hammer when she went to show him the new wig. Just when they were getting used to Rani-ma's horrendous hairdo, the problem was solved by the parrot who obviously felt the shock the most. The bird picked up the offending wig and flew out to the tree outside with it. After sitting on it for a while, it dropped the wig suddenly and accurately into a squirrel's nest and came back chuckling softly. By the time Rani-ma found out, it was too late. The squirrels had torn the hairpiece into fine shreds and lined their nest with the bright red strands. Rani-ma went back to her untidy but normal hairdo and the parrot, now wearing a smug look, settled back on her shoulders again.

The palace was peaceful once again, when suddenly one day a man appeared and asked for Gita. After the guards had asked him questions and cleared him, he was brought to the veranda and presented to Rani-ma. All the women ran to the windows, curious to see who he was, and even Bolubana swayed in to inspect the stranger. Gita could not recognize him at first, he had grown so thin. But his eyes were the same, in fact more dreamy than ever. 'I have come to take you home,' he said in a soft voice, looking down at his feet. 'This is my home now,' replied Gita gently, so that he would not feel too hurt. They stood in silence, not knowing what to say to each other. At home, everyone else had done their talking for them. Rani-ma seemed to suddenly read her mind and she stepped forward. 'Come, son, have something to eat. A train journey makes one so hungry,' she said and offered him a sweet from a basket nearby. As her husband sat down to eat, the parrot flew and settled on his shoulders as if he was an old friend. Gita knew that her journey had ended at last and now her life would begin.

Threads of Revenge

YESTERDAY I FOUND AN OLD KANTHA MY MOTHER HAD STITCHED for my daughter when she was a baby. A pretty one, with green and pink flowers. I remember my mother and my aunt sitting together in the little patch of garden we had—working and talking. They only sat there in the afternoons, stitching kantha quilts from old cotton saris, occasionally sipping tea or getting their feet massaged by the maid who hovered around them. They never bought thread from the shops. 'Waste of money.' They used the coloured threads from the borders of old saris. I remember helping them pull out the threads and getting slapped smartly on my hand when I snapped a thread in my eagerness to yank it out from the border.

One day my aunt, who was visiting us from Kolkata, brought a beautiful embroidered kantha and spread it out in the sunlight. It was an old faded one with beautiful flowers and birds but if you looked at it for a long time strange faces with haunting eyes would stare back at you. I did not like the kantha at all but my mother loved the intricate embroidery that covered it like a web. She never saw any faces lurking in its flowery depths. 'This girl has too much imagination, Meera, it will only lead to trouble later in life,' my aunt warned my mother when I tried to point out the ghosts lurking amidst the flowers and buds.

'My mother-in-law gave this to me,' said my aunt touching the fragile border gently.

'Her family was very rich. Zamindars from Borishal. She brought a huge dowry but her husband, my late father-in-law, drank it all away. My poor husband got nothing at all and I did not even get a pair of bangles from them. Anyway, god has been kind and we are alright,' she said touching her heavy gold bangles with a smug smile. The aunt, each time she came to visit us, told us at great length how rich her husband's mother's family had been. 'Uneducated, feudal bandits,' my father muttered each time she began her tale, and my mother said he was jealous of their immense wealth. They had an army of servants, 200 acres of land and her husband when he was a young boy had a pet goat, a parakeet and a woollen jacket made in England, but the drunkard father-in-law lost everything. I often wondered what happened to the goat and parakeet. My father wondered what happened to their collection of vintage cars.

'All I got from my mother-in law was this old kantha,' said the aunt spreading the frayed cloth on her lap. 'She told me that the kantha had been gifted to her by her mother's sister on her wedding. She had never seen this aunt before and did not even know the woman's name. When she asked her mother she got no answer. She never saw her aunt again.' Many years later when they had all passed on, I learnt where the kantha had come from by stitching together fragments of family tales. The sad faces hidden amongst the embroidery told me the rest.

When Ashima saw the golden envelope she burst into tears. There was no need to cry because it was not bad news announcing someone's death. It was just an invitation to her elder sister's daughter's wedding. She hadn't seen her sister for almost ten years and this daughter ... she must be nineteen years old now. Nineteen years and three months exactly. Her name when she was born was Parul but now they called her Mondira. Ashima wiped the tears from the wedding card which was red, with a bold gold and pink lotus in the centre. It was wrapped in gold tissue paper and tied with a silken thread. Expensive and gaudy. She would have chosen a simple design, maybe a tiny garland of flowers with a faint sprinkling of gold dust on pale orange paper. But she was not the mother. She *was* the mother—but not anymore. She had given her away. No. They had forced her to give away her baby girl 19 years and three months ago.

Ashima hardly ever thought about her baby. She had her sons to take care of, her lazy good-for-nothing husband to worry about, and the house to manage. But sometimes, when the moon shone through her window, making the room bright and harsh and she could not sleep, then the day came back to her.

It rushed at her like a sandstorm, overwhelming her and making her cry out in terror. She watched herself crying silently, counting the minutes, waiting for the pain to end. Then the moonlight vanished and all was calm. She listened to her husband's gentle snores and fell asleep once more, her face wet with tears.

It was late evening when Parul finally came out of her womb, screaming abuses like a fishwife, an ugly bundle of blood and mucus.

'Oh, no, no. We see bad temper here,' said the midwife, spitting out her paan juice. She laughed as she held the baby upside down as if it was a dead chicken. 'I better give her a little slap, just to remind her she is a woman and not a prince who can show his temper to the world.' And then Ashima saw her slap the baby hard on her bottom. She remembered before drifting off to sleep again that her brave little girl had screamed even louder.

Had they made her good-tempered now with regular beatings? Or had they let her grow up, spoilt and wilful? She was very pretty, people said. The only child of rich parents and she would get a good husband, they said.

Ashima had stood outside her school one day, hoping to catch a glimpse of her, but when the bell rang and all the girls rushed out, she didn't know what to do. How would she recognize her daughter? She watched, panic-stricken, as all the little girls ran past her, each one looking like her own flesh and blood.

'Let her go, Ashima. Give her to your sister. God will bless you. She will grow up in a wealthy home, they will marry her into a rich family. You already have three boys. Think of their future. If you please rich relatives it always helps everyone in the family. We will never get a chance like this. This is our moment to have them forever in our debt. Give her away, she is only a girl. They are a burden to the family,' her mother said, stroking her palm, cajoling her.

Her father, usually quiet and mild-mannered, was surprisingly agitated when they came to take Parul away.

'Mamoni ... Are you sure? I do not want any regrets later. You can refuse if you do not want to give your girl away,' he said, but he took care to whisper so that her mother wouldn't hear.

'No, she cannot. She has promised her sister. It was all decided before the baby was born, remember? If it was a girl we would give the baby to her. Ashima will do as we say,' her mother replied. She looked at her husband, a bit startled by his odd behaviour. In the thirty years of their peaceful wedded life he had never raised his voice or contradicted her. 'So the old man still has a bit of fire left in him. I must douse it at once,' she thought and swiftly turned around. Narrowing her eyes into strips of black she aimed them like darts towards her husband. Twisted her mouth in a jagged curve, a formidable combination of a grimace and a smile. It never failed to work. Her husband looked down at his feet and began mumbling nervously. She watched him for a moment, making sure he was his old, obedient self and then said loudly 'So all is decided and we are all happy now.' She smiled at them, picked up the baby and walked out of the room. The door slammed shut.

The door always slammed shut when her mother finished talking. Even now when she was an old woman, muttering incoherently all day to her long dead husband, screaming at people only she could see, Ashima feared her voice.

They gave her baby away nineteen years and three months ago and she regretted it every day of her life. She tried not to think about her, pretend nothing had happened but the pain clung to her, hiding in the folds of her skin, stinging her face. At night suddenly, two small hands would grab her neck, and her face and two tiny eyes would stare at her from the shadows. Sometimes when she was alone in the house, she heard a baby crying.

'You're mad, just forget her. She would have been an extra mouth to feed,' her husband said. 'Look at our healthy, handsome boys. How well they are growing.' Her daughter was a weed they threw out so that their boys could have more sunlight to grow tall, healthy and strong.

She wished she could see her just once so that she remembered her face for the rest of her life, but her mother didn't want her to visit her sister. 'People will talk,' she said. At first her sister sent her letters telling her how Parul, now Mondira, was growing up, sharing small things like her first word ... 'bandhu' ... her favourite food ... 'bananas' ... but then after a few years the letters stopped. Ashima was never invited to visit. The door was slammed shut once more. Her sons were not told they had a sister. Years passed. Nineteen years and three months.

Ashima folded the letter and put the wedding card in her sewing basket. She then took out a deep red thread and began sewing flowers on the soft cotton. She had been making this kantha for her daughter, her lost child, for many years now. She embroidered only at night when the moonlight did not let her sleep. She lit a lamp and sat near the window, making tiny stitches in the cloth, thinking about her child. Sometimes her husband woke up and muttered angrily, but she ignored him and he went back to sleep. This much she had learnt from her mother ... how to ignore a man's temper and make him obey with a tiny grimace, a swift cold glance.

He had never cared for their baby girl. 'Let her go. We will save the dowry money. The boys can have a bit more,' he had said. 'Your sister's husband is so rich, if we please him, he might find jobs for our sons when they grow up,' he added, sounding just like her mother. She sometimes thought they had plotted this together. Sat up at night planning what they would do with all the money her baby daughter would bring. A girl who brought in money was a rare thing; a rare, precious thing, to be bartered only once in a lifetime.

Her sister had been generous with money and gifts. She had paid for the boys' education in a good school, paid for Ashima's operation, for the roof to be repaired, a new Jersey cow, and her husband's new dentures. Her little baby girl had made life easier for everyone but she couldn't do anything to take away the pain which dug its claws deep into Ashima's heart, choking her at night.

She had embroidered sixteen flowers and had three more to do. One flower for each year she hadn't seen her and three tiny leaves for the months. Only she would keep this secret. Her daughter would never know who she was. What would she say when she saw her for the first time? Would her face be like hers, a reflection of her? She would have to be very calm and still when they met for the first time. Everyone would be watching them. There should be no talk. But why would people talk or care? she had asked her mother. 'It is a matter of family honour. I do not want people to say your sister is barren. It reflects badly on me. It shows I have produced a defective child,' her mother said and suddenly burst into tears. 'I only try to do my best for you girls,' she wept, and for the first time in her life Ashima saw sadness in her mother's eyes.

As her fingers flew over the soft cloth, three old saris folded over many times, Ashima suddenly began to embroider a face. It was a small, ugly face with huge eyes and a bald head. A baby's face. A screaming mouth. She tried to turn it into a flower, quickly putting in a plain chainstitch, but the needle seemed to move on its own. Ashima watched her fingers fly, her heart beating rapidly as the images began to form on the cloth. She made a line, a curve and then it moved into a strange shape. Eyes, hands, mouths and bodies appeared as if by magic. She couldn't stop. She tried to make a leaf but after a few stitches the needle ran away from her. She had never worked so fast. The cloth was covered within minutes. There was no place left anymore. Flowers, half-opened buds, garlands, birds, fishes and butterflies danced about and then, hidden beneath them, were faces: her father looking at her helplessly, her husband with a gaping, greedy mouth, and next to him her mother, smiling her victorious smile. In one little corner, surrounded by trees and flowering creepers, stood an empty cot and above it loomed her own face looking out blankly. The faces and figures wove in and out of the flowers and birds. Now a baby emerged out of nowhere—her baby—and crawled all over the soft cotton cloth. Then as she embroidered, the baby grew into a girl. She ran and skipped through the garden, jumping on trees, as Ashima's fingers sewed faster and faster. The thread ran out but before she knew it, the needle had a long, green thread trailing behind it. The needle pricked her finger and it bled into the cloth, merging into the red and orange threads. Again and again the needle pulled the strands of thread as it filled the kantha with tiny, hidden stitches.

Ashima saw her empty house, her sister's grand mansion, her mother's twisted grimace, her boys as old men, and then she stopped. Her head was spinning, her fingers were stiff with pain and she could no longer see clearly. The needle fell from her fingers and was lost in the darkness. The moonlight shone on the cloth which was now covered with hundreds of intricate stitches, each one a breath of her life.

Ashima sat with her head bowed for a long time and when she lifted it up again, it was dawn. Her mother was quiet for once and the house was still. Her sons were away in the city. They worked for her sister's husband. Her whole family were slaves to her sister, who never let them forget it. Her mother said it was good to have rich people in your debt, but she was wrong.

'You were wrong, Ma, for once in your life you made a mistake,' Ashima shouted to the empty walls. 'I will forever be in her debt. I am forever chained to her because she has my child and my heart in the palm of her hand.'

Ashima picked up the cloth. The needle was embedded in it. There was a small empty place still left where she sewed her name but quickly hid it under a curling leaf. She cut the thread off, then laid the cloth aside. She didn't want to look at it anymore. Her sister would open it, the faces would stare back at her and she would know, only she would know, what the kantha said.

She would see the greed in her mother's eyes, her husband's grasping hands, her father's helplessness, and then she would see her, Ashima. Others would see flowers, gardens, birds and leaves, but her sister would see the faces hiding in them. She would feel Ashima's sorrow, share her pain. She would know the story each time she saw the kantha and that would be Ashima's revenge. A small, petty revenge but that was all she had the courage to do after nineteen years and three months.

Ashima bathed, put fresh flowers in her grey hair and then draped her best sari—a gift from her sister—around her. She found a pair of golden slippers, another gift from her sister, and put them on. Her hand trembled when she painted on her bindi and it sat lopsided on her forehead.

Her mother watched her from her bed, spitting out her food and clawing at the sheets with her twisted fingers.

'I am going to Parul's wedding, Ma … Remember my daughter … Parul? You didn't like the name I gave her when she was a day old. "Her new name, Mondira, is much better … more suitable," you said. Suitable for what? For being given away as a gift? Ma … do you remember anything? Does anything matter to you?'

Her mother whined as Ashima wiped her mouth. She gently unclenched her fingers and patted her head. 'Sleep, Ma. I will bring you some wedding "payesh,"' she said as she smoothed her mother's hair. And and then, carrying the kantha, she left the room and slammed the door shut.

A Simla Tea Party

MY MOTHER TOLD ME THIS STORY MANY YEARS AGO ON A DARK and humid summer evening. The electricity had gone off and we were sitting in the candle-lit verandah, slapping away the mosquitoes which stung our bodies with unerring accuracy. My mother and my aunt were fanning themselves with reed fans which were trimmed with brightly-coloured frills that hissed like snakes each time they turned. I preferred a much-folded newspaper square which circulated the humid air more effectively and silently.

'Have you ever had scones with clotted cream?' asked my mother suddenly with a resounding slap on her hand which must have certainly killed the mosquito that landed on her.

'No, I've only read about them in Enid Blyton books,' I answered, feeling hungry all of a sudden. We had just finished a hurried dinner cooked by my aunt who kept grumbling about the 'power cuts', and said my mother was to blame because she had voted for this particular government in the recent elections.

'What you vote, so you reap,' she said each time the house was plunged into darkness.

'I will make scones on Sunday.'

'If NDMC Electricity Department allows,' said my aunt twirling her fan agitatedly.

'Ma, why did you suddenly think of scones with clotted cream?' I asked. My aunt snorted from one corner of the verandah, her white sari gleaming in the flickering light of the candle, making her look like a large moth at rest.

'Why do you laugh, Neelima?' asked my mother and I could hear the smile in her voice though I couldn't see her face.

'You know very well why, Meera,' said Neelima Mashi. 'Greed is a sin but God is all-forgiving sometimes. You certainly ruined my silk bag. I could never remove the smell of stale cream from it however many times I washed it. It was such a pretty bag, with red flowers.' I saw her lift a finger and point aimlessly into the black sky and my mother lifted her face, too. In that blurred, trembling light I saw them staring into the darkness as if they could see clearly into a world which had long gone by; a world still real and animated for them. I realized then that as long as you have someone to share your past with, it never fades away and you can plunge into its sorrowful, comical, dark or joyous depths whenever you want.

Meera wore her best sari, oiled her long hair and plaited it neatly. Today was Mrs Thomas's annual summer tea party. She was not nervous at all. She had memorized the ten English sentences she had to say to the English lady and then she would have all the delicious pastries, which were forbidden at home. Her mother didn't allow them to eat eggs, meat or chicken, and even onions and garlic were banned in their kitchen. Meera loved eggs and could eat three a day if she was allowed to. She sometimes hid an egg or two in the huge hamam which stood puffing and panting like an old war horse in the courtyard. She waited till the water was boiling and then quickly slipped the eggs in. She kept a close watch for three or four minutes and took them out before the servant poured the water into a bucket for her father's bath. She had got distracted one day by a monkey that had jumped on the roof and carried away her mother's spectacles. By the time she came back it was too late to retrieve the eggs. The eggs, hard-boiled by now, had struck her father, bruising his forehead and forming a big lump, which had remained for a long time. She had been punished for a week and not allowed to go to the Mall or eat any sweets.

Meera raced down the hill path, swinging the silk bag she had borrowed from her sister without asking. Her ayah followed her, breathlessly calling out to her to slow down.

Meera looked at the hills and chanted,

'How are you, Mrs Thomas?

'I am very well. Thank you.

'It is very warm today.

'Yesterday was cold.

'It may rain today.

'How is your dog?'

Meera paused, trying to remember if Mrs Thomas had a dog. Last year there had been a puppy playing in the garden but she wasn't sure if it had belonged to Mrs Thomas. It was safer to stick to the garden sentences.

'Your garden looks beautiful.

'These are pretty flowers.

'I like roses. Roses are my favorite flowers.

'Which are your favourite flowers, Mrs Thomas?'

By this time tea and hopefully a variety of cakes and pastries would have arrived.

'Yes, thank you.

'No, thank you.

'It was very kind of you to invite me.

'Goodbye, Mrs Thomas and God Save the King.'

Mrs Thomas's drawing room was large and airy with windows that opened out into a long verandah. A heady scent from the red rose creepers climbing up the pillars filled the air. They could see the mountains beyond. The curtains fluttered in the breeze and the roses trembled and shed red petals on the floor. Meera was glad she hadn't memorized the dog sentence because she couldn't see any dogs in the garden. There was a black and brown cat sitting on the fence but Meera decided to ignore it. She could have asked, 'How is your cat, Mrs Thomas?' but then it might lead to new areas of conversation with difficult English words. It was safest to stay within the familiar circle of conversation they knew.

The pink flowers on the sofa Meera was sitting on looked as if they had faded and died in the summer sunlight. A tiger skin was spread out on the floor and Meera moved her feet away. She could see the place where the tiger had been shot. A small dark hole.

She looked around and smiled politely at the other four girls. She knew them from school but they were not her close friends. Her best friend's mother never allowed her daughter to come to this monthly English conversation tea party. 'We will lose caste and she will not get married.' Her own mother too wasn't keen but her father insisted.

'The girl will learn some table manners and correct drawing room behaviour. She is growing up as wild as a native child. It is very kind of Mrs Thomas to call these girls for a tea party. You should go with her, too.'

Her mother looked aghast and quickly ran into the prayer room before her husband sent her off to an English tea party. It was bad enough that he worked for the British instead of looking after their vast acres of land in the village, like her father and brothers did, and now he was threatening to send her to some nightmarish tea party!

They had been sitting in the flower-bedecked drawing room for half an hour and now only twenty minutes were left. The tea party always lasted exactly fifty mintues. Each one of the girls had spoken their English sentences and now sat looking relieved and happy. Mrs Thomas smiled at them kindly, her faded blue eyes matching the flowers on the sofa, and Meera smiled back once more. Her cheeks were aching now and her stomach growled with hunger.

She glanced quickly at the girl sitting next to her who was silently chewing the lace on her handkerchief. Meera was sure everyone could hear her rumbling stomach.

Then at last the doors opened and the scones arrived floating in an aroma of butter.

'Have some scones, girls. I have just taught the cook how to make them. I hope they're not too hard, our oven is so old and temperamental,' said Mrs Thomas, waving her hands.

Meera didn't know what 'temperamental' meant and she had never seen scones before. She had had many kinds of cakes and pastries at Mrs Thomas's tea parties but this was something new. They looked like tiny cakes which had not risen properly or had been bashed about. There were little pots of jam and cream sitting on the tray. Meera's heart sank as she looked at the misshapen cakes. She was really looking forward to the delicious confectionary they got each time and she was disappointed. 'They are feeding us spoilt, sunk cakes which nobody else wanted to eat,' she thought, gloomily eyeing the scones.

The bearer, tall and regal in his starched uniform and cockerel like turban, condescendingly offered her one but she didn't know what to do. Should she use her fingers or the spoon? She was suddenly panic-stricken.

'Use your fork,' the bearer hissed with a sneer.

Meera picked one up clumsily with her fork and then, as she hesitated, Mrs Thomas quickly took one from the plate with her fingers. As Meera and the girls watched, the old lady slowly lifted her knife, as if it was a magic wand, and sliced the scone into two neat halves. Then she dabbed clotted cream on each half generously and looked up. All the girls were staring at her, their eyes wide open, forks and knives suspended mid-air. Mrs Thomas smiled and nodded at them, then reached for the strawberry jam. She scooped some up with a spoon and spread it slowly and carefully on the clotted cream. Meera quickly did the same. Now the plump buttery scone sat on her plate like a miniature hill, glistening with snowy white cream and wearing a crown of crimson jam. She closed her eyes and was about to pop it into her mouth when the room burst into chaos.

'She has gone … she has been kidnapped!' screamed the ayah as she ran into the room, her white sari trailing behind her like the mast of a drowning ship.

'What! What are you saying?' said Mrs Thomas staring at the old woman who was now slapping her hands on her face.

'Quiet, Ayah, quiet,' she said in a low but firm voice and rose from the chair.

'Keep calm, keep calm, girls,' she said looking at them and then hurriedly left the room. They heard excited voices outside on the verandah and looked at each other anxiously. Meera saw the jam slowly dripping down the scone.

'They say she was walking on the Mall and he just swooped down and carried her off in his motor car,' shouted the bearer. His lofty demeanour had disappeared and he was screeching like a bazaar urchin. The servants now crowded into the kitchen, talking in loud voices, while the girls sat quietly wondering what to do. Through the open door, Meera could see Mrs Thomas fanning herself with a Chinese paper fan, pacing up and down the verandah. Should she quickly pop the scone into her mouth? All the girls were now looking at her and then at their plates. Meera reached for the scone. She pierced it with her fork but it slipped. The cream now swam around the plate tinged with drops of crimson jam. The girl sitting opposite Meera just picked it up with her fingers and quickly put it in her mouth. 'Tastes like a squashed cake,' she mumbled, her mouth full of cream and jam. Then she wiped her hands on her dress. 'Use the napkin, silly girl, use the napkin. Mrs Thomas will see you,' another girl whispered.

'I cannot imagine such a thing happening in Simla, and that too with the Viceroy in residence for the season,' said the English lady who had just arrived in a rickshaw. She was standing next to Mrs Thomas on the verandah. She too was fanning herself but with a reed fan. They kept turning around and looking into the drawing room at the girls.

'These people are very hot-blooded. Anything can set their passions aflame. An ankle exposed ... a bit of shoulder above a low-cut gown. You know, Emma, I never let the dhobhi wash my undergarments, Ayah has to do them.'

'Imagine what Fiona's poor mother must be feeling. Such a scandal, and the season's just begun. I always thought the Maharaja was such a polite, well-bred chap. Spoke English with a proper accent.' said Mrs Thomas.

'All a polished veneer, dear, underneath they're all savages waiting to devour us,' said the other lady fanning her herself nervously. Then she turned around and smiled at the girls through the open door.

Meera understood what they were talking about though she didn't know many of the words. A maharajah had kidnapped an English girl from the Mall. That's what she understood and she told all the other girls present. They didn't seem very interested. The girl who had been chewing her handkerchief now picked up a white napkin and began to nibble at it. She hadn't taken a single scone.

Meera waited for Mrs Thomas to look away and then quickly picked up her plate. The scone winked at her. The cream now flowed down to mix with the jam, making the scone look lopsided.

Meera's hand had almost reached her mouth when Mrs Thomas rushed in, almost tripping over the tiger skin on the floor.

'You all have to leave! I am sorry, my dears, but you must all go home at once. We will do our little tea party another day, I promise.'

'They have called out the police on the Mall,' said the bearer, his turban now sitting crookedly on his head.

Meera rose from the sofa with all the other girls. They all said, 'Thank you, Mrs Thomas,' in one voice and began walking out one by one through the door. Meera stayed back as the girls went out. She picked up four scones and slipped them into her bag. The soft cream, the crimson jam slid down the silk bag as the sirens began to wail on the Mall. Meera wiped her hands on her sari and left quickly.

All the local people seemed to have disappeared from the Mall and the shops were shut, though it was only five o'clock. Meera followed the other girls and they walked in an orderly line although no one had asked them to do so. Suddenly they were all feeling nervous and scared. Meera's ayah was nowhere to be seen.

'What if the maharaja kidnaps *us* now?' whispered the napkin-chewing girl.

'How many girls can he kidnap in one day?' retorted Meera. She could feel the jam dripping through the silk cloth. Should she just eat one now? Mrs Thomas was far away and couldn't see her.

No, the girls would laugh at her. They would call her a greedy thief. She should have eaten the scone at Mrs Thomas's house. Picked it up quickly, sliced it neatly like Mrs Thomas had shown them, spread the cream and topped it with strawberry jam. Now if she took them home her mother would make her throw them away at once. She would have to throw away the silk bag which was now ruined in any case. Her sister would be so angry and her mother even more so.

'God knows what animal they have killed to make this thing, cow, pig or goat. Why did you bring it home?' she would say. She would make Meera wash her hands five times. Three times for the tainted food she had touched and twice for shaking Mrs Thomas's hand.

Meera began to walk faster. Maybe she could hide somewhere and eat the scones before she reached home.

Two of the girls had turned into a narrow lane that led to the Upper Mall. Meera followed them. They reached a corner and suddenly two English soldiers appeared out of the shadows of the pine trees. 'Where are you going to, my beauties?' one of them asked and whistled. Then he laughed and put his hand out to stop them.

Meera began to run. The other girls hadn't noticed the soldiers but when they saw Meera running, they screamed and began to run. 'Ghosts … English ghosts …!' Meera screamed.

'Listen, girls. We were just joking,' the soldier said walking towards them.

'Run, run, they will kidnap us!' Meera screamed again and scrambled up the hillside.

She started climbing up a narrow path and the other four girls followed her, crying loudly.

'Sorry, girls, we meant no harm,' the soldiers shouted from the road. They stood and watched as the girls, led by Meera, stumbled up the steep path. Then they walked away, laughing loudly.

When they reached the top of the hill, Meera flopped down on the ground. Her new sari was torn and her slippers wet with mud. The girls quickly sat down next to her, breathing heavily.

The napkin-chewer was sobbing loudly. 'My mother will kill me for ruining this dress. It cost Rs 150,' she wailed. The others looked flushed and excited.

'Imagine, we almost got kidnapped, too!'

'But not by a maharaja.'

'Yes, but they were English soldiers. Not ordinary black sepoys.'

'But you said they were ghosts, Meera.'

'Could have been. We were very near the cemetery, and you know all those English ghosts lurk there, especially at five o'clock,' she replied.

Meera suddenly felt something wet and soft on her hand and screamed. The other girls began screaming too and the napkin-chewer leapt up and then immediately sat down and began chewing the ribbons on her plait.

Meera looked down and saw it was the silk bag, the jam spilling out. She reached into the bag and took out the scones. They were totally squashed and no longer looked like the elegant little cakes topped with cream and strawberry jam, sitting prettily on a silver tray in Mrs Thomas's drawing room. Meera stared at the mess for a few minutes and as the girls watched, she formed the scones into a big lump with her hands. She had seen the cook knead dough in this way. Then she divided them into little balls and gave a tiny one to each girl. As they sat chewing the strange lumpy pieces, the sun set over the mountains and a flock of ravens flew over their heads, cawing angrily.

'Let's go home now, girls. Next month we'll go to another tea party at Mrs Thomas's and eat proper scones properly,' she said laughing.

What made my mother think of those long forgotten scones, I have never understood. Could it have been the rustling sound of the reed fans or the flowery edge of the cushion she saw in the dim light? What took her back sixty years? I never found out, but I remember that she did make us some delicious scones the next day and we ate them properly, spreading the cream and jam with a knife just the way Mrs Thomas had taught her.

Grandmothers & Ghosts

SARALAMA CAME TO WORK IN OUR HOUSE LONG BEFORE I WAS born. She was very rude and bad-tempered but an excellent cook and could make the most delicious sweets, which my father loved. She never obeyed any instructions my mother gave her, did exactly what she wanted. The other servants resented her and often complained to my mother, but she was helpless. I think my mother was a bit scared of the old woman. Saralama always liked my brother much more than me and fed him all the special sweets she made. She would give me just one and say I was an ugly, wild child who had been left at the door-step by a bandit.

Saralama often told me very scary stories while she shelled peas or cut the stems of spinach leaves. I had to sit very still otherwise she threatened to call my bandit family to take me away. I loved the thrill of these stories laced with the danger of my being suddenly whisked away by my true bandit parents. The story-telling almost came to an abrupt end when my mother found out. 'These stories are giving her nightmares,' she said to Saralama 'Please stop at once. She is only eight years old.'

Saralama did not stop. 'I was married and widowed at your age,' she said and continued to tell me her blood-curdling tales. This one, a true story, was my favourite.

Saralama had heard it from her grandmother who worked in a rich zamindar's house all her life. She went to work there as a young girl and died in the same house when she was very old. Saralama said that she outlived almost all the members of that household. Then, rolling her eyes till I could only see the whites, she said that her grandmother's ghost still roams the house which is now in ruins.

Many years have passed and I am almost as old as Saralama now but every time I pass that house, now a block of flats, I remember Saralama's warning. 'If you don't sit properly when people come to visit, if you don't chew your food well, if you don't let me comb your hair, my grandmother's ghost will catch you. Look, there she is roaming in the old house, waiting to pounce on naughty little girls like you.' I still hope that someday I will see Saralama's grandmother looking down at me from the balcony, her silver, ghostly eyes telling me her story once again.

My sister dragged my hand through the wet darkness. My legs trembled and my eyes watered as I tried to keep up with her long strides. All I could see in front was a snake-like silver path running through the blackness. We had woken up when the sky was still black, dressed quickly and sneaked out of the house like thieves. Though she hadn't said anything I knew my sister didn't want my father to see us leave. Not that he ever really saw us through his lizard eyes, always blood-shot with rage and alcohol. He abused, ordered, shouted and threw things at us, but never looked at us. Our mother had always kept her face covered but I knew that she was always looking at us from underneath her palla. She fed us secretly, sliding bits of food when my father wasn't looking. 'Why do you feed these two so much? They are eating me out of house and home, these leeches,' he would shout if he ever caught her giving us food.

Our mother is dead now. My sister said she lives in the stars with all our other dead relatives.

'Is Ma looking at us now from the sky?' I asked my sister, shouting through the darkness. 'No,' she replied. 'Listen, just keep your mouth shut. When you reach the Kothi, only speak if the old lady asks you something. Get that into your thick head,' she added, digging her fingers painfully into my arm.

I kept quiet but I knew my mother was watching me from a small corner of the sky that night. I looked up at the black sky and smiled at her. I felt safer now in the dark.

'Isn't she too thin and small?' asked the fat old lady, chewing a twig of neem. 'I do *not* like thin servants. They eat too much and cannot lift heavy things. They fall ill a lot and I always worry that they might die in the house. I hate dead servants,' she declared, spitting out a mouthful of green neem juice near my feet.

'No, Mamoni, she may look thin but she is quite strong. She does all the work at home. Cuts grass, cooks, cleans, washes, feeds the cattle and my father,' my sister said in a soft, sweet voice I had never heard before.

'Looks small to me. Hey, girl, lift me up,' said the fat lady raising her arms to me like a child. My sister gave me a push forward and I almost fell, but I knew at once that I had to do this. It was a test for me. If I passed I would have a roof over my head, food to eat and clothes to wear. I would escape my father's blows. My sister never told me all this, I just knew it.

'Come on, girl, don't dawdle. Is she deaf? O my cursed fate … to deal with an insect-thin and deaf-mute at this time of my life,' whined the old woman, her large dead-fish eyes glaring at me. I could feel my sister's silent fear but she didn't say anything. Maybe she too felt I was too thin and weak. Maybe she was thinking she should have left me with my father to cook, clean and be thrashed every night.

No, I was not going back, ever.

I took a deep breath and caught hold of the two arms which were almost touching me now, the white flesh wobbling, ten fat fingers twitching. I caught hold of each arm, they felt as heavy as a log of wood but they were so soft and smooth that I was worried they might slip from my grasp. I pulled, closing my fingers tightly around the two fat arms. I shut my eyes, pretending they were branches of a dead tree on which a wicked, evil witch lived. I had to pull the branches, uproot the tree with all my strength otherwise she would come down and gobble me up. I pulled and I pulled till my heart was in my throat.

'Aiiieee … Baba re … You are as strong as a bull! You little wretch,' shouted the fat lady and laughed as she staggered to her feet. She was just a little taller than me but as round and heavy as a sack of rice. I looked at my sister. She was smiling too. I knew I had passed the test, everything would be alright now.

That was three years ago. I know because I can count now. I learnt from the books the children of the house scatter on the table after their tutor has left. I dust them carefully, though they are shiny and new, with a wonderful, fresh smell unfamiliar to me. I make sure I dust the study when the tutor is here every morning so I can repeat in my mind what the children of the house learn. Two and two make four, three and five make eight, I repeat as I scrub the floor and wash the dirty clothes. I count till two hundred every night as I lie on my cot.

They do not know what I know and they hardly see me as I go around the house. I am invisible to them unless they need something. The children, two boys, are always throwing their clothes, toys and books on the floor, then shouting at me to pick them up. I spit in their milk when I fetch it from the kitchen, that is my little victory over those wicked creatures, though it doesn't make me feel any better.

My sister and I live in one corner of the Kothi, in a small room next to the cattle shed. She gets up at five, wakes me, and then we sweep the courtyard, milk the cows, clean the shed, light the kitchen fire to make a huge cauldron of tea. My sister gives me a glass of milky tea with some leftover rice and after we both eat, we rinse our mouth with water several times because the old lady sometimes checks us. 'Open your mouths, you greedy bitches. I don't trust you village girls, you eat like buffaloes.' We are not supposed to eat before them, though the cook sometimes gives us leftover food which we hide in our room. Occasionally he even gives us a piece of fish which we eat at once because if we hide it, it will start smelling and give our secret away.

Now as the sun rises over the rice fields and the lonely, one-eyed cock in our courtyard crows mournfully, we carry cups of tea to the family. There are five cups of tea, and some round things called biscuits. I have never tasted one and would love to take a small bite, but my sister says she will cut my hand off if I do.

I am going to have one, one day, when she isn't looking.

First room we go to is, of course, Mamoni's since she is the oldest member of the family. Her husband, called Dada-baba by everyone, is older but he is totally insane and hardly ever comes out of his room. When we go in to clean the floor and make the bed he shouts and tries to grab us. Once he caught my sister's arm and pinched her. She hates him but I think he is so funny to look at, like an owl with big ears. I like playing a game with him, dodging him as his claw hands fly at me. It was a game I played at home with my sister, running around the bed. I laugh and let him tickle me, but my sister slaps the old man's hand and pulls me away.

Then one day I have an idea. I tear up an old sari, one that even we cannot wear anymore, stitch it and stuff it with soft cotton wool from an old mattress. I shape it into a small ball. I take this with me, hiding it in my sari when we go to clean Dada-baba's room. I wait till my sister is on the other side of the room, then I swing the ball into his face. His eyes light up and he quickly grabs the soft lump of cloth. I let him, then pull it away. He laughs and almost jumps out of the bed. I don't want to excite him too much in case he starts shouting. My sister is still busy on the other side of the room, so I let him catch the ball. He hugs the cloth ball to his chest as if he is a girl playing with a doll. He smiles at me sweetly, his ears twitch, and then he goes to sleep.

'The old man is quiet today,' my sister says as we leave the room and I just smile to myself.

I realized that day that men are easy to please. A little scratch here, a tickle there or just give them something soft to hold and they're happy. I am old now and almost blind. Dada-baba is dead and so is Mamoni, and the two sons. All are stars in the sky. The daughters-in-law are somewhere in the house. I hear them calling me but I cannot seem to find them.

My daughter takes care of me and them too. I cannot remember my husband's face, whether he was a kind or a cruel man. I hear his voice sometimes, but then it could be my father's voice.

The old woman is all around me, hissing at me through the decades. I can see her through my blind eyes, walking around my room, wheezing, farting as usual, muttering abuses in a low voice.

As I sweep the stairs I can hear her shouting at him, calling him a dog, heap of dung, rat, snake and many other things. Sometimes he shouts back but I can't understand what he is saying. 'He is shouting in English, Dada-baba had an English tutor when he was young. Now he has forgotten everything—his children's names, even his own name, but he remembers many English poems,' the mali's son told me. He knows everything about the house since his father and grandfather have been working here all their lives. He gives me guavas from the garden which I eat in the afternoons when the household, including my sister, is asleep. I feel so hungry all the time, a strange ache sits in the pit of my stomach like a curled fist, and I eat the guava leaves too.

Mamoni sips her tea noisily while I press her feet, kneading the flabby flesh like soft dough. 'Not so hard, you imp. Your hands are like wood. There … there, near the ankles. Oh, my feet ache … They get so tired,' she moans in between quick slurps of tea. How can her feet get tired when they hardly walk at all? They go from the bed to the durrie on the floor and then back just once a day. We carry her, bathe her, and even clean her bottom.

My mother's feet were like two pieces of dried wood but she never complained of pain, never asked me to press her feet. I wish I had, quietly at night, when my father was asleep.

The old lady sighs and dips the biscuit thing into her tea. Then gives a loud fart which goes on forever. We both listen to the rise and fall of the whine as if it was a song and then, finally, it ends. She smiles at me as if she has done something wonderful and we must all clap our hands and bow. She dips another biscuit into the tea. My mouth waters and I swallow quickly. Maybe she will leave a bit in the cup. But when I check later, the cup is empty. The greedy, old woman has swallowed it all up, tea, biscuit, even the grains of sugar that sometimes remain at the bottom of the cup for me to lick. Hope her stomach churns with pain. Tomorrow I will give her a bruise when I press her feet.

We go to the next room to serve tea to the older son and his wife. He is a serious, quiet man with a sad, long face like an old donkey in our village. He is always reading big fat books and doesn't mind if I look at them when clearing the teacups. His wife, fair, plump and very pretty, talks to us all the time, showing us her clothes, jewellery, various parts of her body. If she has a pimple we have to examine it closely. Though I often think she is not really talking to us, just talking so that she can hear her own voice, breaking the silence of the room.

'Do you think my one breast is smaller than the other?' she asks me, lifting up her blouse as her husband reads the newspaper. I stare at her flat chest not sure what to say. 'They look the same to me, Bodobouma,' I mutter, bending down to pick up her slippers which have overturned. It brings bad luck, my mother used to say. 'What more bad luck can God send me? Two daughters and a shrivelled up wife,' my father would laugh if she ever said that, throwing his slippers at her.

Bodobouma lifts her sari palla, her heavy gold bangles jingling loudly and asks me again. 'Tell me girl? I know for sure one is bigger than the other, though I can't tell which is which,' she says with a giggle as she sips her tea. Her husband grunts and turns the page. My sister gives me a kick which means, move on.

After this we go to the younger son's room. There is music blaring from the radio, clothes strewn all over the floor, half-eaten sweets, open paan boxes, cards, dice and stale garlands of jasmine on the bed.

Pictures of babies with golden hair are stuck on the dusty window. I love this room though my sister calls it the worst room in the house to clean. 'How can two people make so much mess?' she grumbles as we sweep, dust and swab the floor, fold the clothes and make the beds.

The younger son, a tall handsome man with curly hair and large, bulging eye like his mother, and his pale, sickly wife lie in bed all day, arguing. We often have to wait in the verandah till they get up so that we can make their bed. 'Let it be, girls, let this cleaning be. We'll mess it up again, won't we? Come, play cards with us,' the younger son says. He is the only one who talks kindly to us and never abuses us. Sometime he strokes my arm absentmindedly when I pass by. I don't mind it and I would love to learn how to play cards, but my sister shakes her head and waits near the door with her broom in her hand. Her tight, angry face shows what she thinks of them. The elder brother's wife often joins them on the bed and the three of them play cards all day while we serve them tea and snacks. Sometimes when I am sweeping the room, I see the younger son stroking the elder wife's back, his fingers moving under her blouse. Maybe he is checking which breast is bigger. The elder son never comes into this room.

Listen. I can hear them now shouting in the other room. Why don't they just sit quietly in peace, wait for their time here to finish. What is there to fight about now? I want to go to them but my legs are too weak and my eyes only see shadows. I used to be so strong, picked up the old lady every day to bathe her.

I lean against the wall, smell the food rotting in the courtyard and I remember the feast day.

Today is the old man's 90th birthday and though he will not come out of his room we will have a grand feast in his honour. Four kinds of fish—rohu, hilsa, prawns and papda—a meat pulao, seven vegetable dishes and five different kinds of sweets. The cook has made a big fire and extra boys have come from the village to help him.

When the cook told my sister the menu my mouth began to water. Maybe we will get some leftovers today. Surely they cannot finish all the food?

The family bathes and gets dressed early. I run from room to room carrying buckets of hot water, polishing the sons' shoes that are covered with dust since they are worn so rarely. In between all this fetching and carrying I oil and comb the daughters-in-law's hair, put out garlands of flowers, and then finally I wrap Mamoni in her stiffly starched sari and prop her up on the bed. She gives me a sharp kick in my shin when I try to arrange the sari over her legs, and laughs.

When I turn to go away she cries, 'Come here, you lazy slut. Stay near me.' I bathed her alone today since my sister was busy helping in the kitchen and she is so pleased with me that I am to bathe her every day now. I hate it. Her flesh is like a rotten potato, soft and white. I am afraid to touch her naked skin. I know that worms will come out of her body and crawl over me. I poured water over her quickly and threw the towel over her head. Then I lifted the heavy, slippery body from the floor to the bed and dressed her. 'Sprinkle more talcum powder. In the folds, in the folds,' she said in a sleepy voice. The rose-scented powder tickled my nose and I felt a little calmer.

The old man, Dada–baba, whose birthday we are celebrating, is also bathed and dressed like a bridegroom in a dhoti and white silk kurta. He lies on his bed like a corspe ready to be taken to the funeral pyre, a marigold garland around his scrawny neck. He lifts one arm suddenly and waves to me. Now he looks just like his younger son. Maybe he wants to stroke my arm, too.

I run out of the room.

I walk in the shadows along the corridors, sticking close to the wall, taking care to make myself small and invisible so that no one can ask me to fetch or carry something. The aroma of food stuns me as I walk into the main kitchen where the cooks are stirring three huge cauldrons. I never knew food could smell so rich, so heavenly. I felt dizzy with hunger and greed.

Now I know what the stray dog in our village feels like when it watches us eat, a line of drool hanging from its jaws.

'Here, girl, take this to the priest. He has to feed the gods before anyone eats. Hurry, hurry,' the cook pushes a small silver thali towards me. I stand still not sure what I should do.

'Do you think she should touch it?' asks the second cook looking down at me. His bare chest shines with sweat lines as if someone has poured oil on his skin.

'She looks young enough to be clean,' says the head cook peering absentmindedly at my breasts though I do not have any as yet—only two bumps like mosquito bites.

'Are you clean, girl? Do you bleed?' asks the first cook, throwing a handful of chillies into the cauldron of hot oil.

I want to sneeze but control myself.

I hang my head not sure what they are asking me. The fragrance from the cooking pots is now seeping into my skin and my stomach growls so loudly that I am afraid the men will hear it.

'Let her carry it, I'm not walking all the way to the top floor, my feet are like lead now,' says the main cook. He is a kind man who gives us leftover food sometimes but we have to scratch his back with a neem twig in return.

The puja room is on the topmost floor of the house. The priest chants here all day and then brings the dhoop down along with the prasad for the family, twice a day. The door, a brass one with lotus leaves, opens into one corner of the terrace where coconut palm trees lean over and pigeons rest in the afternoon. We are not supposed to come here, though Mamoni sends me here sometimes to check if the priest is praying. I am to tell her if he is asleep. He is snoring gently on the marble steps most of the time, holding on to the tiny brass bell as if it was a rattle, but I never tell the old lady that. Let the gods decide if they want to punish him, why should I bother? Moreover, he often gives me stale fruit left over from the prasad. It smells of dhoop.

Today there is no one inside the puja room. Then I look again. The priest is fast asleep as usual. The food on my thali begins whispering to me. I had ignored it so far, tried not to inhale as I walked up the stairs to the temple. If I held my breath the fragrance would not be able to torment me. My stomach growls with hunger. My mouth fills with saliva. I am drooling like a mad dog.

'Taste just a bit.'

'Try only a morsel.'

'Eat, eat ... no one can see you.'

I pick up one handful of rice. I have never tasted rice like this. It is fragrant, sweet yet salty, melting in my mouth.

I will only eat the rice and nothing else. Gods don't want rice.

It is not my hand that is picking up the food and putting it in my mouth, yet I feel the sweetness, the saltiness. Each morsel lingers on my tongue and then slowly melts in my mouth. This is really food for the gods.

I can hear the priest snoring as I finish all the food on the silver thali. There wasn't much. The gods in the temple watch me eat. They don't say anything, don't strike me dead.

But I know when the priest wakes that I will have to pay the price. He will thrash me and then my sister will beat me. I will be sent back to my father who will also thrash me just from habit.

I look at the empty thali and begin to pray for the first time in my life.

The gods don't answer. I walk down the steps slowly, already feeling the blows on my head, but my stomach is full for the first time in my life. It is a strange feeling, not to be hungry. The gnawing pain in the pit of my stomach has gone. My greed has vanished. I don't care if they beat me. I feel content, like Dada-baba with his cloth ball.

Then as I race down the steps, my stomach starts to ache. I stop. I don't want to be sick, want to keep the food in my belly forever. I feel a warm, stickiness between my thighs. I touch myself and my fingers are red.

I am not clean. I am not pure. I am not a girl anymore. Now I understand what the men were saying. I must have been bleeding when I picked up the silver thali.

How could I have carried the food to the gods? It was tainted by my unclean hands as soon I touched it. They would never have eaten it. The fragrant, tainted food wasn't meant for the gods, it was meant only for me.

Today as I walked past the place where Saralama's grandmother's ghost lived, I noticed a shamiana had been put up. Several huge cauldrons of food were laid out and a line of people were being fed. I raised my eyes to the balcony, and in the gathering dusk I saw a figure shimmer. I knew she was coming down to taste the food. I hope she likes it. I closed my eyes and prayed that the demons of hunger have left her now that she no longer has a body and has merged with ether forever.